Christmas Stories

For

Children and Adults

By

Margaret McBride and Barry Smith

Cover art painted by Margaret McBride

Thank you to Char Torkelson for editing and formatting.

This book was printed in the United States of America.
Copyright © 2016 Marbar Creations, LLC

ISBN – 10: 0-9916045-7-1

ISBN - 13: 978-0-9916045-7-9

TABLE OF CONTENTS

NOWTHEN

"Grandpa, tell us a story, please!" Burt Randolph's three grandchildren begged as two of them sat on the floor before the old stone fireplace. Each of the children had a snugly blanket wrapped around them even though it was warm in Grandpa's cabin. The blanket was a present their grandfather had given them for Christmas and was embroidered in big letters that said: "JESUS LOVES YOU."

"I'm not sure I have any stories left that you have not heard," Grandpa Burt told his grandchildren. He sat for a few seconds rocking back and forth in his homemade rocking chair with his eyes closed. "Well, maybe there is one you might like to hear. Do you remember the winter I went to see your other Grandpa and Grandma?"

"You were gone a longtime Grandpa," said seven-year-old, Barbara. "You stayed with Grandpa William and Grandma Emma while they were sick. You even missed Christmas with us, didn't you?"

"Yes, I did stay a long time and something very interesting happened while I was there. What year was that? Hmm, 2012, I believe it was."

"It is 2016 now, Grandpa," mentioned eight-year-old Marcus.

"Yes, I believe it is. What do you think, Jennifer?" Grandpa Burt asked his nine-year-old granddaughter. She had her blanket wrapped around her inside her wheelchair.

"I don't know," was all Jennifer answered with a sad sound in her voice and her eyes downcast.

Jennifer was her Grandpa's broken heart, not broken for himself, but broken for her. He prayed for her every day, and he promised himself that for the rest of his life, he would see to it that each and every Sunday, she would have a way to church. A bicycle accident had put her in a wheelchair, and she had been unable to walk since that dreadful day. Now, he was afraid that she had given up and was no longer even going to try to walk.

"Well, where am I going to start this story?" Grandpa Burt said as he again rocked back and forth. Glancing from one of his grandchildren to the next, he smiled before he spoke. "Your other Grandma and Grandpa live in a town with a very unusual name. It is called Nowthen. The community of Nowthen is north of Minneapolis, Minnesota where they have lots of farm land and lots of horses."

"I had been with Grandpa William and Grandma Emma for about a week when I heard about a big black horse one of the neighbors owned. They said he was a mean critter, and would stomp anyone who got close to him. Mean as all get out, they said."

"I remember that it was very cold outside, and a pretty good snow had fallen the day before Christmas, perhaps this high." Grandpa Burt raised his hand above the old wooden plank floor to show his grandchildren how deep the snow had gotten. "Grandma Emma was disappointed because she and your Grandpa, being so sick, would miss Christmas Eve services at church, something they had not done in 50 years."

"It was snowing that evening, and not only was the snow getting deeper, the weather was also becoming much colder. Sitting by the fire, I heard a loud noise coming down the driveway. Then, there was a knock on the door. Answering the door, I saw the county sheriff covered in snow, standing out in the cold. He was traveling on one of those snow machines they have running all over the place up there in Minnesota. The reason he was out in such bad weather was because he was notifying everyone that the big black horse had gotten out of his corral and was asking everyone to keep an eye out for him. While the sheriff was standing there talking to us, we heard an excited voice over his portable radio. 'Sheriff Carter, come in. Come in, Sheriff Carter. We have an emergency,' I heard a voice say. 'You need to get over to the Swanson's place. Little Patty Swanson is missing.'"

"I then heard Grandma Emma behind me say, 'Oh my goodness! That sweet little girl, Patty, is missing out in this awful cold.'"

"Now, Patty is a member of the church where Grandma Emma and Grandpa William go, and they had known her since she was born. She was only twelve years old, but she sang in the church choir, and according to Grandma Emma, she was as smart as anything. The next thing I heard was Grandpa William saying, 'If she's out there in the cold, there is one thing I know about that young lady, and that is, she will never give up until she is home. Never, never, never!'" Grandpa Burt glanced at Jennifer.

"The snow continued to fall, and Grandma Emma and Grandpa William wanted to get dressed and go look for Patty, even though they were as sick as could be. It did not matter to them. They still wanted to go out in the cold and join the search, but I would not let them. As much as I wanted to go myself, I just couldn't do it because I was looking after them."

"'Burt,' Grandma Emma, told me, 'I've got to do something. I can't just sit here and do nothing!'"

"'Emma,'I said, 'If you tell me what to do, I'll make some food for those people who are out looking for her. We'll call someone and have them take it to the church. There will be a lot of people out there searching for her tonight, and they will need something to eat.'"

"So, that is what I did on Christmas Eve. Grandma Emma told me what to do and I made the food for those out looking for Patty. As it turned out, every woman in Nowthen must have had the same idea because the church was loaded with food. Every man capable of hiking in the deep snow or riding one of those snow machines was part of the search. Some were even on skis going through the forest and all of them needed to be fed.

But Patty was not found that night. She had disappeared, and we feared that she was buried under the snow. As it turned out we were right."

Grandpa Burt looked over at his grandchildren. Mark and Barbara's eyes were open very wide and were glued to his. An expression of sadness was on their faces. Glancing at Jennifer, Grandpa Burt saw that her eyes were still downcast, but he could see a tear rolling down her cheek.

"Grandpa, I don't want to hear anymore about your story," Jennifer said softly.

"But Jennifer, it is time for a happy ending," Grandpa Burt said. Jennifer's eyes darted up to her grandfather's face.

"Grandpa William said that Patty would never give up, and she didn't. Now here is what happened."

"When Patty left the house to check on her Shetland pony, it was snowing, but not very hard. She thought it would be a perfect time to go out and make sure he was all right. She did not tell her parents what she had decided to do because the barn was not that far away. After all, she would be right back."

"Patty found that the snow was deeper than she thought, and it was a struggle to get to the barn. The pony was fine, but once she started back to the house, it was snowing so hard Patty couldn't see which way to go. The little girl soon realized that she had somehow gotten herself turned around."

"Grandpa, I'll bet she was really scared," Jennifer said. Grandpa Burt knew he had his granddaughter's full attention and that she now wanted to hear all of the story.

"Patty was scared, all right, and didn't know what to do. It was getting colder, and she told herself she had to go back to the barn and wait for her father. Turning around she saw that the tracks she had made in the snow were disappearing. They were being filled in by the blowing snow, and now she didn't know where the barn was either."

"Grandpa, I don't want to hear any more of the story," Jennifer moaned.

"It's a good story, child. Are you sure you don't want to know how I know all these things about Patty? Let me finish. I know you will like the ending."

"By this time the entire population of Nowthen was out looking for Patty, but the storm was just as bad for them as it had been for her. Nothing could be seen though the blinding snow. Eventually some of the older folks had to stop searching, and all they could do was pray that God would watch out for their little friend. Even though she was only twelve years old, Patty believed strongly in God, and she was also very smart. Her father had taught her not to give up on riding her pony, not to give up on the school work she didn't understand, and most importantly, not to give up on herself."

"'What would Daddy want me to do? What would God want me to do?' Patty asked herself. 'They would want me to find a place to get out of the cold.' Turning

6

around, Patty was still unable to see in any direction but all at once she saw a big dark shape coming toward her out of the blowing snow. It scared her so badly she turned to run away, but instead, fell into the deep snow. When she was able to stand, Patty realized there was a big black horse not more than few feet from her."

"'Are you lost too?' Patty asked the horse. She reached out, brushed the snow off its nose, and touched his head. Placing her hand on the horse's neck, Patty tried to take a step but again fell. This time she could not get up. The snow was too deep and she was just too cold, but Patty was not going to stop trying. Finally, she was able to stand, and, as the horse began to plow its way forward through the snow, Patty hung onto its tail and was able to follow for a short time. Then she fell for the last time."

"There was a lot going on around Nowthen. People were coming in from other small towns in the area. Everyone that could search was there, but no one found Patty that terribly, terribly cold night."

"The next morning was Christmas morning, and I was sitting at the kitchen table, with a smile on my face. It had just come over the radio that Patty was back with her mother and father, but no one knew how she got there. The story she told everyone was that Santa Claus had brought her home after his reindeer found her curled up in the snow next to a big black horse who was laying down beside her."

"I know it sounds kind of strange, but during the early morning hours, I could not sleep, so I stepped out onto the porch, and I saw him. Right there in front of me was Santa Claus with his reindeer. Stopping in front of the house, he asked if I knew where a big black horse belonged. He said that the horse was not on his list and that he needed a little help getting him back to where he belonged. I told Santa Claus that the horse belonged on the next farm."

"Grandpa, you talked to Santa Claus?"

"Yes, I did, Mark."

"'I guess I had better make sure this fine animal gets back to his farm,' Santa told me. 'It sure did a wonderful thing protecting Patty from the cold. She never gave up though. Not for one minute.'"

"'Santa Claus, can I take a picture of you for my grandchildren?'" I asked him."

"'Well' he said. 'I'd prefer you didn't take one of me. I have been delivering presents all night, and do not look my best at the moment. However, you can take a picture of my reindeer and give it to Patty when the time is right. She had a wonderful time flying with me. Tell her I'm proud of her for believing that she was going to be okay. Sometimes it just takes time before something wonderful happens. To believe is half the battle when you want change in your life. You just cannot give up on believing.'"

"While I was taking several pictures of the reindeer, I noticed something odd. All of them were standing on top of the snow, along with the horse. He should have been up to his belly in the white stuff, but he was not. He, like the reindeer, was standing right on top of the snow. When I finished taking pictures, off Santa went to take the black horse back to his barn. I'll have to admit that it seemed very strange that the reindeer, the sled, and even the horse left not one track that I could see. I stood for several minutes watching Santa disappear. Then a flash of light swept across the sky. I got a good picture of it and could readily see Santa riding in his sled as he crossed over your Grandma Emma's and Grandpa William's house."

"Grandpa, you're just making up a story, aren't you?" said Jennifer.

"You see that desk over there," Grandpa Burt said. "You just wheel yourself over there and get me that big picture album."

"I can't do that, Grandpa. It's too big, and I'm in this wheelchair."

"Sure you can. Like Santa said, all you have to do is believe you can do it. Just pick up the album, place it in your lap and bring it to me."

Jennifer wheeled herself over to the desk and tried to pick up the picture book. "Besides that, Grandpa, it's too heavy, and too much trouble."

"Do you think it was too much trouble for all the people of Nowthen to stop what they were doing to go out and look for Patty? Or too much trouble for Santa Claus to take the horse back where he belonged? Or too much trouble for me to tell you a really wonderful story even though I thought you might not believe me?"

"God sent Jesus to teach us to believe in Him and ourselves. If all we want to do is tell ourselves what we can't do, then how are we going to be able to tell ourselves what we can do? There will always be things in this world that we might not be able to do — but that doesn't mean we shouldn't try. You know, Jennifer, God gave us the ability to choose what direction we will take our lives."

"Patty could have given up on herself, but she did not. She made the choice to trust in Jesus. She was not going to let failure take over her mind, just as I think you will not allow defeat to rule you."

"But what if I fail, Grandpa!"

"Fail in what? Not learning to walk again? Child, your doctors have told you your body is ready to walk. If you fail, it will be because you let your fear control you, and you don't trust yourself or the Lord. Give it a try, and you will see that no matter what happens, Jesus will be with you and provide you with the strength you need."

Jennifer thought for a few seconds before she placed her hands on the top of the armrest of the wheelchair. "Not so fast," said Grandpa Burt. "You have to do it when someone is standing beside you."

"I thought you said that Jesus would be with me?"

"Yes, I did, didn't I? Well, He's right there, and I'm beside Him," Grandpa Burt said as he walked over and stood next to Jennifer. Jennifer placed both of her feet on the floor, and with both hands on the wheelchair, she tried to lift herself up but got only half way before she sat back down.

"Pretty good for the first try," Grandpa Burt said. "Remember the choice is yours."

Jennifer tried again, pushed with all her might, and lifted herself up for the first time in two months. Sitting back down, she smiled at her Grandpa. Then she reached over and tried to pick up the picture album. It took her three tries, but when she brought it to her Grandfather she could not believe her eyes at what she saw inside that big album. The reindeer's nose was red just like in the stories and songs of Christmas.

A CHRISTMAS PRESENT FROM SARA

Eight-year-old Sara sat in her room surrounded by eleven of her closest friends. She knew all their names, what they liked to wear, and what they wanted to be when they grew up. Each one was dressed for the day in accordance with what they were going to do that week, and all her friends liked to do different things.

Her friend, Andy, wanted to be a doctor. So today she had put on his doctor's clothing. Mary wanted to be a nurse, and today Sara dressed Mary in all white. Sandra wanted to be a country-western singer, and she was dressed in cowgirl clothing. But in all her collection of dolls, Tina, dressed in her princess dress, was the prettiest doll she had today.

Every Saturday morning, Sara would get up early and start her routine all over again, dressing each of her dolls in different clothing according to what they wanted to be that week. Putting different clothes on all her dolls was Sara's most favorite thing to do. It was also a wonderful day when her mother would let her go with her to garage sales so that she could look for more dolls and doll clothing. Her mother would spend her Saturday driving from place to place looking for good deals from people who no longer had a need for some of their items.

Sara was well aware that her parents did not have a lot of money, so she would help her mother in the kitchen or take out trash and even help her father in the yard when her older brother was gone. She might earn only a few pennies or maybe even a nickel or dime for her help, but that was okay as long as she earned something. Sara saved all her money until she felt she had enough to go looking for another doll.

It was only two weeks before Christmas, and Sara wanted to have all her dolls see the beautiful lights displayed in their neighborhood. She made sure each of her dolls had their chance to sit on her windowsill so that they could see all that was going on outside.

Sara had all types of dolls from just a few inches tall to her stuffed doll that was almost as big as she was. It did not have to sit on the windowsill because he was tall enough to look right out the window when he was standing up. Her bedroom was a doll heaven with all her "friends" lined up in neat rows along every wall.

That next day, after Sunday morning services at the church, Sara found a tear in one of her doll's dresses and asked her mother to show her how to sew so she could fix it. Not only did they fix the dress, but she and her mother also made a new dress for her doll. Sara found that sewing was not an easy thing to do, but after a few tries she was able to sew another dress for one of her other dolls. It was not as good as the one she had made with her mother, but Sara knew her doll, Priscilla, would be proud of it nevertheless.

Going downstairs after changing her doll's clothing, Sara heard her father talking about a big storm that had gone through a neighborhood not far away. Her father said how lucky they were that the storm had not destroyed their neighborhood also. Three days later, as Sara's mother was taking her to see one of her friends, a detour had to be made around the area that had been damaged by the storm. They stopped several times to look at the destruction that was everywhere, and at one place, Sara saw a little girl crying in front of a home that had been destroyed. In the little girl's hand, Sara saw half of a little doll. Its clothing was gone, along with one arm and leg.

Sara knew how the little girl must feel because she had broken one of her dolls once and cried for days when it could not be repaired. With both the arm and leg missing Sara knew the little girl's doll probably could not be fixed.

When Sara's mother drove her home, they again passed by the damaged houses. Sara thought about the child who must have felt like her world had come to an end and felt sorry for her. Christmas was rapidly approaching, and she was certain that all the little girl's dolls must have been destroyed.

"Mother, is there anything we can do for the people who lost their homes?"

"I wish we could, but we have so little ourselves, I don't know what we could do for them," Sara's mother told her.

When Sara got home, she went upstairs and counted her money. It was only $1.20.

"Can I find a doll for this much?" Sara wondered. Maybe she could get her mother to take her to some garage sales the next Saturday. There was no snow, but it was really cold, so maybe there wouldn't be any sales for Sara to go see. Going to her mother, she asked her to check the papers to find a garage sale.

"I'm sorry, Sara, but there aren't any garage sales this time of year. Don't you have enough dolls already?"

"I wasn't going to buy one for me. I was going to try and find one for the little girl we saw the other day who had lost her dolls in the storm."

Sara's mother stared down at her daughter. "What a wonderful thing for Sara to think about doing," she thought. "I've heard that there are a few places that have indoor sales. Why don't we see if we can find one of those? Maybe they will have a doll or two for you to look at." Sara's mother checked the paper for one of those indoor sales.

"Sara, they're having a rummage sale at the county fairgrounds this Saturday. It is the last one of the year, and it's in the big exhibit building. I'll bet we can find a doll there. I'll take you to see what we can find." Sara's mother was so proud of her daughter for wanting to help the little girl, so how could she say no.

Sara waited anxiously for Saturday, hoping she would be able to find a doll for the little girl. Sitting among her own dolls, she looked at each and every one.

"I'm sure the little girl is very sad today. Everything she had is gone. If I can't find a doll for her, one of you will have to go to a new home. I am very sorry, but there are so many of you. I do not want to give any of you up, but she has none. I hope you will forgive me for giving one of you away. I love you all, but I don't know what else to do."

Sara set all her dolls around her. "Okay, which one of you would like to have a new home with another little girl?" She picked up each of her dolls knowing that she might lose one of them. "I love every one of you," she said again.

Sara got up early on Saturday morning. The sale started at 9:00 AM, and she did not want to be late. Her mother had promised that they would be on time. The fairgrounds were big, and Sara saw that the building where the sale was going to be, was huge. People were everywhere, even on this cold winter day, and the place was packed. Tables were placed so that all she had to do was walk down each row looking for a doll to buy. Finally, she saw one, but it did not have any clothes on.

"How much would you like for this doll?" Sara asked the lady behind the table.

"Honey, it is only two dollars because it doesn't have any clothes.'

"That's okay. My mother has taught me how to sew. Can you let me have it for $1.20? That's all I have."

"Oh, I'm sorry, honey, it's $2.00," the elderly woman said.

Sara sadly walked away. The lady saw the disappointment on Sara's face.

"I'm sorry," the woman said to Sara's mother.

"That's alright. We stopped and looked at the damage the storm had caused, and Sara saw a little girl crying because she had lost her dolls when her house was blown apart. Now Sara's trying to buy her a new one for her Christmas. She thought your doll would be good because she is becoming very good at making doll clothes now."

The elderly woman stood for only a few seconds looking at Sara's mother before she picked up the doll and walked around the table. Passing another table, the woman stopped and spoke to a man looking over the items being sold. "That little girl over there is Sara, and she is trying to get stuff for the people who lost everything in the storm." Leaving the table, the elderly woman walked up to Sara. Kneeling down, she started speaking softly to her, "Your mother told me what you are doing. Here, you take this doll, make some clothes for it, and give it to the little girl for Christmas."

"Oh, thank you. Here is my $1.20."

"No, you keep your money. You just make some nice clothing for the doll, then you and I will both make her happy. Okay?"

The man at the table watching all this, walked up and set a box on the floor, "Here is some clothing my daughter once wore. If they do not fit the little girl, I'm sure there will be someone else they will fit."

Word spread like wildfire that a little girl named Sara was collecting dolls, clothing, toys and anything that might help those whose homes had been destroyed, making it possible for them to have a Christmas. Anything that people wanted to give should be taken up to the front door.

Sara and her mother could not believe what was happening. A man arrived and put a ten-dollar bill into Sara's hand. Boxes of toys and clothes began stacking up. Coats, shirts and pants and hundreds of other items started arriving from all over the building. People were giving generously and none held back. In addition, over $1,000.00 in cash was given to help those whose homes had been destroyed.

"Here, Mother. We have to give this to the people, but, who do we give it to?"

Items were still arriving when the man who had given Sara the first ten dollars, returned. "I know that you are going to have to find a way to get this stuff to the school where the storm victims are staying, but don't worry. I called my friend who works at City Hall, and he has a large truck on the way."

"Excuse me sir, but who are you?"

"Paul Sherman, I run the newspaper, the Mansfield Daily. I'm the owner and its only reporter. It's just a small local paper, but we're going to have a great headline Monday morning!"

Everything was picked up as Mr. Sherman said it would be, and on Christmas Eve it was delivered to the school auditorium, to those still waiting to return to their homes. On Monday morning, the headline in the local paper read:

"A TOWNSHIP CHRISTMAS"

"This is the happiest story I've been honored to report all year. It took the compassion of a little girl to open the hearts and pocketbooks of a lot of adults, making this a wonderful and happy holiday for many storm victims who were not going to have a Christmas. They will always remember this year and "'A Christmas Present from Sara.'"

On the night before Christmas, Sara walked into the school auditorium with only one thought in her mind. She had to find the young girl she had seen standing in front of her destroyed home, crying for her little doll. Sara pulled a wagon and in it was the doll she had made and the seven boxes she had found on her doorstep the day after word had spread about her mission. There was a note with them asking her to share them and personally give one to the little girl whose home had been destroyed.

"There she is, Mother. I'll take these to her." Sara did not know what was in the boxes, but she guessed it had to be dolls.

"Hi, I'm Sara. What is your name?"

"Sally," answered the little girl.

"These are for you," Sara told her. "I didn't want you to not have a Christmas." Sara then reached into the wagon and took out the doll she had gotten from the rummage sale and said, "I made the clothing for this doll just for you."

Sara guessed the little girl was around six years old. She was very shy and still sad about the loss of her doll. Her mother stood next to her, her eyes filling with tears. Reaching out, Sally did not say anything, but she took the doll in her arms and looked up at Sara, smiling from ear to ear.

Sara took the other boxes out of the wagon and gave them to Sally. They sat down together as both mothers watched. In each of the boxes, which had never been opened, was a brand new Barbie doll.

Sally was thrilled with her new Barbie dolls, and laughed as she carefully examined each one. Then she put them all back into the wagon, including the doll Sara had made for her. She took hold of the wagon and then Sara's hand and started walking among the many families who had found refuge in the school gymnasium. Sally saw a small girl and stopped. Reaching into the wagon, she took out one of the Barbie dolls, handed it to her, and said, "Merry Christmas." The little girl smiled and hugged the doll to her heart.

Sally walked throughout the auditorium taking Sara with her, looking for other small girls and giving each of them one of her new dolls. Sara was sure the little girl was going to give away the doll for which she had made the clothes, but when all the Barbie dolls had new owners, Sally stopped, reached into the wagon and picked up the last doll. Turning back to Sara she said, "Thank you. This one is mine. It is the best one of them all!"

When Sara got home, there was another package by the front door with a note that read:

"Hi Sara. I watched as you gave the little girl all the Barbie dolls. I also watched as both of you made seven other little girls so very happy. Merry Christmas. This one is for you!"

Love,
Santa Claus

TODD

The chilly winds of December cut through my clothing as I stood in the doorway of the mission. Outside the entrance, my eyes caught the first hint of the heavy, wet snow that was reported to start falling that day. The dark cloudy morning gave me the feeling that the snow would continue throughout the day.

A woman and her little girl tucked in heavy winter coats appeared out of the snowfall. Walking down the frozen sidewalk, the two kept their heads low to keep the blowing snow out of their faces. Leaving her mother, I watched as the little girl sped up on the icy sidewalk and stopped to look into a store window. She stood there for a few moments without saying a word. She must have known I was there, but I had become invisible to her, as had the rest of the world with her eyes glued on what she saw behind the glass.

I continued to watch, wondering why the girl was looking into the window for so long as a shiver went through my body from the cold. I heard her say something in her small voice, but I could not understand her words as the wind blew them away.

Having just finished eating a free meal at the small annex of the "Mission Church for the Homeless", I was feeling good for the first time in days in spite of the cold. One of the serving volunteers had mentioned that the weather was going to get a little warmer on Christmas day.

The little girl turned and hurried back to grab her mother's hand. Pulling her toward the window, the little girl pointed at the glass. I was able to hear the mother's words as she tried to explain why she didn't have enough money to buy her daughter what she wanted for Christmas. Stepping away from the window, the little girl hung her head as they turned toward me.

"I know, Mommy. I was just hoping," said the small voice against the freezing wind. I saw the sorrow on the mother's face as she looked down at her daughter.

"Maybe next year," the woman said.

When they walked by, I was still standing in the doorway, and the mother gave me only a glance, but the little girl looked up at me and smiled, "Good morning, sir. Merry Christmas."

"Don't talk to strangers," I heard her mother say.

"Mommy, he's not a stranger. We see him every day. He must work in the church, don't you think?"

"Your mother is right, little girl," I thought. "You should not talk to strangers." But, the girl had helped me through my days by saying "Good morning" whenever she saw me standing in the doorway of the mission. I had seen the same child many times as her mother walked her to school. She had never failed to say "Hi" or "Good Morning" to me. It was the best part of my day, after having my morning meal at the mission.

"To have someone recognize that I even exist in this world makes me feel good, even if God has forgotten about me," I thought.

I said, "Why?" turning to look up at the cross hanging over the door before I started to make my way down the street in no particular direction. I had asked that same question every morning, but like always, I received no answer.

The small hand pointing into the shop window came to my mind, and I wondered what the little girl had been pointing at. Walking over to the window, I brushed away a small accumulation of snow and saw a small doll sitting in a rocking chair. I had already suspected what it might be, and sure enough, that is what she had been pointing at. Opening the door to the store, I entered. Stopping just inside because I didn't want to get snow all over the floor, I spoke to the sales clerk not far away. "How much is the little doll you have displayed?" I asked.

"$19.95," the clerk answered as she looked at my somewhat ill-fitting clothes. I think she was wondering why I would even be in her store. I'm sure it must have been apparent that I hadn't had that much money in a long time, which was in fact the truth.

I had lost my job a year earlier when the company I worked for closed down. After my unemployment ran out and what little savings I had were gone, I lost my car. Then, I was evicted from my apartment because I couldn't pay my rent. I guess I was one of the lucky ones because I didn't have a family to follow me out into the streets. If I had really thought about it, I really couldn't blame anyone but myself. It was easy to think that what I had would always be there, so I had not prepared properly for my future. Now it was easier for me to blame God for my poverty.

Of course, I tried to find a job and get myself settled, but with no luck. My church tried to help, but there were other people who were worse off than me, and I couldn't see taking money or food away from a child or whole families who needed it more than I did. So now, I was eating one meal a day at the mission and still trying to find a job. But, without appropriate clothing to help me look presentable, who was going to even consider me for a job? I guess God really had forgotten me.

I always thought God was someone to lean on during hard times and I guess that is true for some people. But, I had leaned on Him during my good times and maybe He just got tired of it. Who knows where I'd be if I hadn't given so much of my money to the church and toward helping others. Maybe I would have had enough money to keep my car and my apartment. Now, look at me with no future at all. Again looking at the cross over the door, I wondered why my life had turned out this way. "What is it that you put me on this earth to do? I've spent so many years trying to serve you. How is it that I have failed?"

Christmas would be here in only a week. I could feel the tears run down my face as I turned and walked away from the window. The joy of Christmas, at least for me, had disappeared. To be alone on what I used to feel was the most special day of the year was devastating. My dream of Christmas was gone, just as the little girl's dream of having one little doll of her own was gone.

What is it about Christmas that makes us want to give? He gave his life for me, and now all I feel is pity for myself. Why did I even go into the store? Even if the doll had only cost a dollar, it was still beyond my means.

Walking down the frozen sidewalk, I tucked the gloves I had been given into the coat I had also been given — given to me when it wasn't even Christmas. I needed to leave the shelter. It was a place where people like me survive only through the generosity of others — a place where no one knows or cares that I'm willing to work and care for myself — a place where I went after God had forgotten me and left me alone and hungry.

Walking down the sidewalk, I could see colorful Christmas decorations on the fronts of the stores. Stopping on a corner, I looked up, and a light far off in the distance caught my eye. It was a big beautiful lighted star sitting on top of a building. It reminded me of the Three Wise Men's star, and a feeling came over me that the star was calling me as it had called them. I couldn't help wondering why it was even there, because I'd learned that God wasn't making miracles in this world today. I could see that because of all the suffering everywhere around me.

Still, like the Three Wise Men, I followed the calling of the star. It was pulling at me as I walked through the cold wind and blowing snow. The walk was long and it turned out that the star was further away than I thought, but I felt that I shouldn't quit walking. I needed to see if the light really was from a star, or just from the lights on the building. My feet were getting cold, the wind cutting through my clothing, and I wanted to stop. I had to ask myself what I was doing, because it had taken me over an hour to get to the lighted building.

Looking up, I saw there was no star, just a large building with lots of lighted windows. What had I seen when I stood so far away? I was sure it had seen a bright star with its rays shining directly at me. My trip had been for nothing. When I turned around to leave, I saw that the building's lights were being reflected onto the ground floor windows of another small store, then bouncing across the street into an alley, illuminating a large dumpster.

Walking into the alley, I saw the light shining directly into a dumpster. I was not so desperate that I had to go dumpster diving in hopes of finding something I could sell, but still I lifted the half-opened lid. There was nothing unusual in the pile of garbage inside, but as I started to turn away, I caught a glimpse of a shiny object directly in the path of the light. I lifted the dumpster's plastic lid up a little higher. At first I couldn't figure out what I was looking at. It looked like a very small open hand, directly in the path of the light.

I didn't want to touch the little hand because it was shining like the star that I could no longer see above me. The hand was so small that it looked like the moon shining at its brightest on a very dark night. I wanted to reach out and touch it, but I was afraid. Was the reflection shining on the hand for some purpose? I hesitated, but then reached out toward it. "What am I doing?" The thought that this might be some sort of magical happening crossed my mind, but I'm too smart to believe in that stuff anymore. Still, I couldn't stop myself. I had to at least touch the little hand.

Removing my glove, I reached out and touched the small hand. It was cold, a hard cold that felt almost like fire. I now had to get it. I picked it up only to realize that it was nothing more than a plastic doll with its head missing. No wonder it was in the dumpster. I was now on the more privileged side of town, and the child who discarded this doll must have had dozens more. The loss of this one with the missing head probably meant nothing at all to her.

Dropping the doll back into the dumpster, I walked away. I had gone three blocks when I turned to look back in the direction of the building. I could again see the star shining brightly. I needed to go back. In my mind, I could picture the little girl who had wanted so much to have the doll in the shop window. She had a dream for Christmas that wasn't going to come true, and I was walking away from half of that dream.

I hurriedly went back and pulled the headless doll out of the dumpster. All at once, I felt warm inside because I had an idea. What if I were able to make the little girl's dream come true? It was a wild idea, but perhaps it would be possible, if I could find some help.

Returning to the mission, I went in and headed for the crowded dining hall. "Hey, friend, I need some help," I said to the first person I came to.

"We all do," was the response I received.

"No, you don't understand. There is a little girl, and all she wants for Christmas is a little doll. Look, I've found one, but it doesn't have a head. I need a head for the doll. Do you have any idea where I might find a head for a doll? Can you help me?"

"No, I am sorry, young man, but maybe Bill can help you. He used to be a wood carver. Can I see the doll?"

I took the little plastic doll out of my coat and showed it to the old man who looked up at me with sad eyes.

"I once had a daughter with a doll about this size," he said. "I gave it to her the year before she died."

I saw a tear roll down Bill's face as he thought back many years to what he once had. Handing me the doll, he turned and walked away.

I felt sorry for the old man. "Yes, we all have our sad memories, especially this time of year," I thought.

I walked over to some of the other tables thinking, "Maybe I can find this guy named Bill."

People, having just come in from the cold, were sitting around the tables trying to get warm. I knew the mission usually closed after breakfast, but someone had eased the policy allowing the homeless a few more moments of warmth before they had to go back outside. Even with all the distress that filled the room, I could hear laughter and signs of good will.

Walking up to the first guy I saw, I said, "I'm looking for Bill."

"I'm Bill, can I help you, young man? I don't have any money if that's what you need."

"Are you Bill, the wood carver?" I asked.

"Well, I used to be, but I did it only as a hobby. After I lost my left hand, I had to give it up. Why are you looking for a wood carver?"

I took out the doll and showed it to him.

"I need a head for this doll." I said.

"I can't help you. I couldn't help you even if I wanted to — only one hand." Putting his arm on the table, I saw that Bill was worse off than I was. His hand and half of his arm were missing. "Used to have a small business, and I was also a farmer before this happened. Now, I'm nothing," Bill said.

"Okay, I did what I could. Now there was nothing more I could do for the little girl. Her dream will stay just a dream. Maybe next Christmas her mother will be able buy her a doll," I thought.

"Maybe you can carve it," Bill said. "Sure hate to see that little doll's body go to waste."

"Me? I've never carved a thing in my life."

"We've all got to start somewhere. Why don't you give it a try! First we need some wood. Basswood is best for carving, but we can get it done with white pine if we have to. There is a lumber yard a few blocks away. Let's you and I go down there, and maybe we can talk the guy out of a piece a scrap wood. Why are you doing this anyway?"

I told Bill about the little girl and how I found the doll without a head. He didn't say a word until I had finished. Then smiling broadly, he said. "Come on, we will need a lot of time if we're going to get this done. We have to have some other things too, like paint and doll clothes."

All at once, Bill was like a man on a mission. He wanted the little girl to have her doll for Christmas as much as I did. As we left the mission annex, he started telling me how he had gotten to this point in his life, and his story was a lot like mine. Hard times had caught up with him and he couldn't find his way out.

The icy wind cut through our clothing as we walked the two blocks to the lumber yard. Bill had no glove, so I gave him one of mine for his hand, explaining that I could put my ungloved hand in my coat pocket. I could tell that he was grateful because his coat did not have pockets.

When we entered the lumber yard, there was only one clerk present. We asked him if we could go through their scrap lumber pile to see if we could find a suitable piece of pine for carving a doll's head. We explained that we wanted to give a special present to a little girl for Christmas.

The owner must have heard our conversation because he came out of his office. Staring at us for a few seconds, he asked us only one question, "You gentlemen carve wood?"

"I used to, but I had an accident and had to stop. It was more of a hobby than anything, but I did enjoy it a lot. I'm going to show this young man how to carve a doll's head, so we can make sure a little girl will have a Christmas."

"Come into my office for a minute. I'd like to show you what I have carved for myself. I've even sold a few over the years," he said.

"What a beautiful carving!" Bill said as he looked at the owner's desk. "It must have taken you some time to finish it. That's really fine grained hard wood. Not easy to work with and really slow going."

"I see you know your wood," the owner said, holding the beautifully carved Mallard duck.

"Like I said, I used to carve some," Bill said.

"What's your name?" the owner said as he looked at Bill. "Seems like I've seen your face someplace."

"Bill," he said.

"You're not the Bill who carved ducks and won the blue ribbon at the state fair thirteen years in a row are you?" asked the store owner.

"That was a long time ago, before this," Bill said, holding up what was left of his arm. "I'm done with that now."

"You know your picture still hangs on the wall at the fair. You beat me every time I entered. I'm really sorry about your hand."

"Thank you, I appreciate that, but we came here hoping to be able to go through your scrap lumber pile to find a piece of soft pine so I can show this young man how to carve a doll's head."

"I'm Paul Henderson. This is my lumber yard," the owner said. "Bill, I'm going to be nosy after I give this young man enough basswood for a few tries at carving that head. Meanwhile, just give me a minute." One phone call to his clerk, and I was handed several pieces of basswood by the yard man.

"Okay, let's get down to business. Bill, if you don't mind me asking, what got you to where you are now? I am asking for a good reason, but I'll understand if you tell me to mind my own business."

"Not much to tell. I was a farmer and also had a small business selling my carvings. I have no family, and when you lose your arm, there's not much future in being a farmer or a wood carver. I got behind on the mortgage and could no longer pay for the farm, so here I am."

"And how about you, young man. You want to tell me your story?"

"My name's Todd Randle. I was an inventory specialist for the Marksman Willis Company. When they went bust, so did I. Couldn't find another job, exhausted my savings, lost my car and apartment. I still haven't been able to find myself a job and like Bill, here I am."

I concluded by telling Paul Henderson about the little girl; the star I saw above the building; finding the doll without a head, and meeting Bill.

"Hmm, God sure works in mysterious ways, doesn't he?" said Mr. Henderson. "Go and make your doll's head and give it to the little girl. When you both are finished, I'd like you to come by and tell me how it went. Would you do that for me?"

Neither of us were sure why Mr. Henderson would want to see us again, but we agreed. And what was that he said about God working in mysterious ways? Why was he even talking about God anyway?

I'll have to say, carving a head was not easy. Three cut fingers later, and a lot of patience from Bill, we finally got the doll finished. Hearing our story while we were carving the head, the director of the mission supplied the paint we needed for the face. A homeless women hand-sewed clothing for the doll, and real blond hair was supplied by one of the mission's volunteers. The only thing missing was the little girl.

The following Wednesday morning, just before the beginning of the Christmas vacation in the schools, there was a larger than normal crowd on the steps of the mission. The people who relied on the shelter for a decent meal had overheard what Bill and I were up to and stood outside the front doors, anticipating the arrival of the little girl. Once the mother and her daughter were spotted coming down the frozen sidewalk, the rest of the homeless emptied the mission along with all the mission volunteers.

Waiting there was even a camera crew from the local TV station to see the little girl receive her Christmas doll from the homeless people of the city. The mission had contacted the local TV station to let them know how the very desperate still had enough love in their hearts to make sure that a little girl would have her dream come true at Christmas.

All the young girl could do was hold her doll in her arms and cry. Looking up at her mother she said, "See Mommy, I told you that Santa would not forget us." Of course, the mother cried as we all did.

The local papers carried the headlines: "WHY HAVE WE LEFT THEM BEHIND? Perhaps the homeless population of our city has more compassion than those who have their Christmas inside a warm and comfortable home."

The article went on to tell of how the homeless put together the effort to ensure the little girl had her Christmas even above their own needs. She wasn't the only one who received Christmas because Bill and I did go back to see Paul Henderson.

"Sit down," he told us. "I read in the paper how your doll turned out for the little girl. That was a wonderful thing that you did for her." Mr. Henderson looked directly at Bill.

"Bill, there is an opening at the local community college for an instructor for a new course that is supposed to start next month on wood carvings of the world. I've read the book you published years ago on the subject of antique wood carvings. After our little meeting about getting some wood for the doll's head, I took your book to the college. Winning the state fair for so many years didn't hurt, and with your BS degree in agriculture, you would meet the educational requirements to be an instructor. Bill, did you ever try to teach wood carving?"

"No, I never gave it much thought. After losing my hand, the farm, and my enjoyment in life, I just gave up."

"Well, after the school board members went over your book, they felt that you would be qualified to teach the subject and have offered you an interview for the job. It would only be a temporarily position, but could lead to other opportunities. It's not your hands they want in the class, it's your knowledge of carving. It is not an accredited class, but there are 54 students who want to take the course, and the college has had to delay the class because they could not find a qualified teacher. There is an indication that there are many more who would like to take the course in the future. So, what do you say? Having a world-class wood carver is something that our college needs. You never know, maybe it will lead to something more permanent in the future. There are a lot of colleges all over the country that are looking for a little diversity in their school curriculum. Even if the courses are not accredited, I think you will find many students interested in your knowledge."

Bill started laughing. "Look at me! Does it look like I'm dressed well enough to go into a classroom?"

"That won't be a problem. Our church has a program where we get people ready with clothing for job interviews. When you walk into that college, you will look like a professional, ready to go to work."

All Bill could do was say, "Yes." Even if the job was nothing more than temporary, it would get him back to talking about something he loved doing for so many years. With his knowledge of wood carvings, he could indeed have a future. As for me, I also was provided with enough clothing to look good for the job interview I had been offered. A company CEO had read about the little girl, and he sent someone to locate me. After I had an interview with him, he said he could use someone with my creativity and perseverance.

The paper had interviewed me about how I found the doll. When they went to look at the building there were no lights. It was nothing but a dark office building and there was no shining star. That star that had shown me the way to a broken doll and a new future was gone. In fact the owner said that the building never had any lights on it at all during Christmas.

God indeed heard me, and perhaps has been doing so for a long time. I just wasn't listening when He answered.

"MERRY CHRISTMAS, LITTLE GIRL," I thought. "God has kept his faith in me and has shown me that I can still trust in His goodness. He had prepared a road for me to follow, but I had to learn to see it first. As for you, Santa, you will live in her heart for many, many years to come."

SANTA

It was the evening before Christmas, and my two children, their mother Lien,   and I were sitting in our living room. It was the time for us to read the poem "'Twas the Night before Christmas" written by Clement Clarke Moore in 1822. The tradition of reading this poem started in my family when I was only ten years old and riding in the back seat of my father's car.

"Dad," my nine-year-old son Andy said, "We know the poem. You have been reading it to us every Christmas. Why do we have to do hear it again?"

"Andy, the Christmas we celebrate in our family is about the birth of Christ, but many people have been observing it in other ways throughout history. People in many parts of the world start remembering it during Advent, a month before His birth. This poem is one of the ways our family likes to celebrate the holidays. We give presents to each other because Christ gave us the most important thing He had to give, His life. In many countries, including ours, there are legends about saints or mythical characters who bring gifts to good children. In this country, Saint Nicolas or Santa Claus as we now call him, are our symbols for the love and sharing of Christmas. I think that is why Mr. Moore wrote us the poem."

"Dad, there is no Santa Claus. I saw you putting presents under the tree this morning," Andy said to me.

"Yes, there is! I saw him. He was here last Christmas," my five- year-old daughter Tiffany said.

"Yes, that's true, Andy. You did see me put something under the tree." Standing up, I went over and picked up the new Bible I had tucked under the branches. "I wanted this to be yours. It's not really a Christmas present, but it is something I wanted you to have."

"Don't I get one too?" ask Tiffany.

I went back to the Christmas tree and retrieved a new Bible for Tiffany. She gave her mother and me the most wonderful smile. I knew she would take care of her new Bible until she could read all about its wonderful teachings. Going to Sunday school had already helped her learn a lot about God and His Son.

"So, you think there is no Santa Claus?" I asked Andy. "Well, I think it is time I told you and Tiffany a true story about me and Santa Claus." I looked over at Lien, and she smiled. I had told her this story only once. She had smiled then also. Lien had wondered if the story could possibly be true - that is, until my mother and father told her their part in it.

"My belief in Santa Claus disappeared on the night before Christmas when I was only seven years old. I had not gone to sleep because I knew he would arrive, and I stayed up waiting for him until it was late. Hearing a noise downstairs, I knew he would be next to the tree placing presents all around. Creeping down the stairs, I saw not Santa but my father placing presents under our Christmas tree. I found out it was my father all those past years and not Santa Claus. My father was playing Santa Claus. He was the Santa I had believed in for so many years. When I realized the truth, I cried myself to sleep. I then knew that Santa was not real at all. It had been my father all this time and my dreams were shattered. But, that is not the end of the story."

"I look back on that time years ago as if it were yesterday. I decided that I never wanted to see my father put presents under the tree again. Two years later, following my discovery that Santa was my father, the whole family was headed across Nebraska on our way to your great-grandma and grandpa's farm in the far western part of the state for the holidays. What a wonderful time we were going to have opening up our presents and eating all of Great-Grandma's wonderful Christmas treats."

"I was sitting in the back seat trying to read Mr. Moore's poem when I looked out the car window, and oh, what a sight I beheld. There were miles of flat fields covered with snow as far as my eyes could see. It was like being in a snowy white wonderland. When we left Minnesota, there had been no snow, and I was disappointed because I was sure there would be no snow for Christmas. However, as we entered Nebraska, we saw it had snowed earlier, and after only a few miles, a white blanket covered everything. It was like a fairyland. Occasionally I could see brown areas where the wind had blown the snow away, and I would think of them as areas of sadness because they were not enjoying the beauty of the snow as I was."

"Above us, the sky was a beautiful blue, but off in the distance, a line of dark clouds covered the horizon. We had just pulled away from a gasoline station where we stopped so my father could get another cup of coffee."

"I think Father means Grandpa," Tiffany leaned over to whisper to Andy.

Andy gave Tiffany a sour face as he glanced over at her, and Lien smiled as I continued.

"I remember that as we got back into the car, the wind felt colder as it blew up the sleeves of my thin jacket. While we were at the station, I saw those dark clouds in the distance, but now, looking out the front window, I saw they were much closer. Instead of marveling at the vast expanse of snow covered fields and the distant cloud formations, I began to feel very nervous. As we continued driving down the road, the sky turned darker. We were not far from the station when suddenly everything turned pure white, and I could not see a thing out of my window. Dad had already gotten the car turned around. And we were headed back to the gas station. 'I can't see the road,' I heard my father say to my mother, just as a huge gust of wind pushed our car off the highway."

"Suddenly, I felt as if I were back at the park, going as high as I could go on the swings. It wasn't so much like going up and down, but the feeling of rolling over and over as our car skidded off the road. I remember thinking that somehow we were back at the carnival turning over in one of those scary rides I liked to go on. The car stopped its rolling, and I could hear nothing but the roaring of the wind."

"Thank goodness the car was sitting right side up, but getting my seat belt off was not easy. During those moments, as I was struggling to unbuckle the belt, I thought about my mother and father. They were very quiet. Once free of the belt, I managed to crawl over the things that were all around me in the back seat. I thought I had seen my mother and father flying around in the front. They did not have their seat belts on and only moments before, I had reminded them that if I had to have my seat belt on, they should have to wear theirs too. Now, it looked as if my mother and father were sleeping with Mom's head on my father's shoulder."

"'Mother! Dad! Wake up,' I cried to them. 'Wake up, please! I'm scared!' Even at nine years old, I knew my mother and father were hurt. After a long period of trying to get them to wake up, all I could do was cry. I tried to look out the window, but the wind was still blowing and everything was white. I could see nothing at all."

"'Dad,' I said, as I placed my hand on his and felt how cold it was. It was becoming so cold I could barely move, even though I had managed to get my big winter coat and gloves off the floor. I took all the rest of our clothing from our suitcases and covered my mother and father with them. I knew that if I was getting cold, they were also because they did not have their winter coats on."

"As I looked out the window into the white nothingness, I suddenly saw a light high up in the sky. 'It must be from the gas station,' I thought. I wanted to stay with my parents, but I was so cold and the light at the station was calling me. I knew I had to get help because now there were little ice crystals forming on the inside of the car's windows."

"The wind had blown the snow away from the door of the car, so I had no problems opening it, but the only thing I could see was the bright light. There was no sky. I could not even see the snow below my feet. There was nothing but whiteness everywhere except for the light above my head. I knew it had to be the light from the gas station."

"'I have to get to the station to tell the people about Mom and Dad,' I thought as I took my first step. I took another step, and then another towards what really did look like a star up ahead. First, the wind was at my back, and then it began blowing right in my face as if it were trying to stop me from moving forward. I could feel the snow beneath my feet, but I couldn't see it. I could feel the wind as it tried to keep me from going towards the star that was now calling me to come to it."

"I do not remember much of my time walking after that. I do not remember how long I tried to make it to the star. I don't remember falling, but when I opened my eyes, I knew I was not in the same place as I had been before. I was no longer out in the cold. I was warm, yet I could see that there was ice all around me. I was in some kind of building entirely made of ice. Looking up, I could see the star above my head. I could see right through the roof and walls of the building as if they were crystal clear. The light was shining so brightly and extending its rays so far that it disappeared off into the distance."

"Beyond the icy walls, the world seemed to be full of moving color. Brilliant reds and greens were everywhere. Yellows and purples were shinning so brightly I could hardly keep my eyes on them — pinks and orange, blue and gold. Every color that there ever was shone and made up the walls of ice. The light moved up and down and side to side all at once, while changing into new colors that were more beautiful than the last."

"My winter coat and gloves had been removed and in their place, I had on green pants, a red shirt, and purple shoes. The toes of the shoes curled up and had red around their soles, a small bright white light shown straight out from each one. The lights looked just like the star above my head, but much smaller."

"Even though I was in a strange place, I was not afraid. Somehow I knew my mother and father were safe, and I did not need to worry about them anymore. But where was I? Why wasn't I with them? Then from behind me I heard a small voice. 'Hello. I'm Marcus.'"

"Turning around I saw a funny little man about three feet high. He had long sharp ears, a little round hat on his head, and bright colored clothing."

"'Who are you?' I asked the little man."

"'I told you, I'm Marcus. I am a trainee, and now I'm in trouble with Santa.'"

"'What do you mean you're a trainee and in trouble with Santa? Who's Santa?' I asked."

"'Boy, you're sure a dumb one. Oops! I can't say that any more since I've become a trainee at Santa's Workshop. You don't think he accepts just anyone to work for him, do you? You have to go through the program and pass all Santa's requirements. It sure isn't an easy job getting everything right for Christmas. You would be surprised how many parts go into just one toy car, much less a toy naval aircraft carrier with almost 200 pieces. I have to learn all that!'"

"'What are you talking about?' I asked, as the little man looked up at me."

"'Okay let's get this straight,' he said to me. 'I've waited for over two hundred years to get into this program to help Santa with his Christmas toys. I only started last week, just seven days before Christmas. He had more requests than normal this year and needed a little more help to get things ready for tomorrow, because as you know, he has to deliver all his presents the night before Christmas. That's how I got to come over and help. I thought for sure I could show him that I was the one he wanted to keep, but then you come along and mess things up for me.'"

"'I'm sorry. I didn't mean to mess things up for you.'"

"'I know you didn't. I was testing the light for Santa's reindeer to be sure they could find their way back if the weather doesn't clear up. I saw you fall and didn't have enough time to get you back to your car, so I had to bring you here. Now, I find out that I should have dropped you off in a place where you would have been found right away. I'll never pass the trainee program now. When Santa finds out what I've done, he'll send me back home and I don't blame him. I should have known better, but being a trainee, I didn't know what to do.'"

"'Is there anything I can do to help you keep your job?' I asked him."

"'Yes, put these on,' said the funny looking little man as he handed me a pair of rubber ears that looked just like his — long and pointed on the end. I placed them up next to my head, and they fit perfectly over my ears."

"'Now, all you have to do is put on this hat and come with me. If any of the others ask you where you are from, just tell them, my home town,' he said."

"'My home town? Where is that?' I asked, as I was putting on a huge hat that had some kind of rubber ball on the end that hung almost down to the floor. The hat was red and blue with gold stars all over it."

"'I have no idea where your home town is located and neither will they, but whatever you say will be acceptable to the others because they are all too busy to ask many questions. You will be just another one of the new helpers on the line, a new guy on the block, you might say. I'm going to show you what to do until I have a chance to get you back to your mother and father. You ever make any toys before?'"

"'No. I'm only nine years old,' I told him."

"'Okay, I'll show you, and you can help me. By the way, when Santa Claus comes around, get down on your knees so that you don't look so tall. You are much taller than the rest of us.'"

"'But why are you trying to fool Santa? That is not very nice, you know,' I told him."

"'I'm not. Santa Claus cannot be fooled. But, if he finds you here, he will take time out from his inspections to get you back home, and he just does not have the time today. Besides, I am the one who brought you here, and I think it is my responsibility to get you back where you belong. I might not get to keep my job as Santa's helper, but I sure don't want to make him late delivering his presents. That would make a lot of kids very sad tomorrow, and I do not want that on my conscience. Also, Santa would be very unhappy with himself. From now on, you have to stay until I can return you to your parents. You are going to be one of Santa's elves.'"

"Daddy, were you really one of Santa's elves?" asked Andy.

"Actually I was more than that. I got to work with Marcus all over Santa's village and I was there for a very long time. However, time in Santa's workshop was not like it is here for us. When I got back, it was as if I had been there for no time at all."

"You were in Santa Claus' workshop?" Tiffany asked. She had a questioning look in her eyes thinking that I might be joking.

"Yes, I went with Mr. Marcus, who I later learned was Mr. Marcus William Handfield Jr., to the toy line. He was right. I was taller than the hundreds of elves who were standing on the line watching each finished toy quickly moving across a long table. I couldn't even tell where the table started or ended. There were toys of all colors and sizes mixed together, and I felt there was no way I was going to be able to do whatever it was that Mr. Marcus Handfield said I needed to do."

"'Okay, Dillon you are looking for only one kind of toy. When you see it, make sure it has a blue top on it. If it is blue, then you have to catch it like this.'"

"Mr. Handfield's hand shot out, and he caught a blue toy truck. 'You see this? It is supposed to be in the other line for the kids who want Santa to bring them a truck that's painted blue. This blue truck somehow got put on the wrong line. Go ahead, you try it.'"

"Somehow I couldn't get my eyes to focus on all the toys going by. Other elves were catching toys, but after an hour I had not caught even one. None of the other elves on the line had looked at me because I was taller than they were, but when I couldn't catch even one of the blue trucks, every eye, up and down the line, turned and glared at me."

"Then I saw a blue truck. Everyone else had missed it because they were looking at me. It was small, and I knew I had to have my timing just right as it went by or I would miss it. 'Wait, wait, wait,' I told myself. 'Now,' I said and shot my hand forward, but the little blue truck had gone by so fast that I didn't have a chance to grab it."

"'The new guy is not doing his job,' I heard someone say."

"'Give him a few more minutes and he'll get it,' Marcus told them."

"There! I saw another one, only this time I didn't wait so long. When I brought my hand back, I held a small blue truck. Every elf as far as I could see was allowing toys to go by while they clapped for my first success. I got pretty good at catching blue trucks, but then everything became a jumble as Santa Claus came walking down the toy line inspecting everything that went by. I remembered what Marcus had said and got down on my knees, so that I wouldn't be so tall. Santa Claus stopped right in front of me. Mr. Marcus must have been nervous because he missed the truck, but I did not."

"'Very good,' said Santa. 'Mr. Handfield, you should have Dillon show you how to do it.' Then he looked down at me and smiled. 'I'll talk with you later, along with Mr. Handfield,' Santa Claus said. 'Now you can stand up.'"

"Santa started walking down the line of toys again, stopped, turned around, and said. 'Nice ears, Dillon,' and then he looked at Marcus."

"'Oh!' said Marcus, 'Santa will think I was deceiving him by not bringing you directly to him, but I didn't want Christmas to be late for so many children because of me. Oh, well, I guess it is back to my home town after Christmas.'"

"I remember feeling bad for Marcus. He had saved me from the cold and had told me that my parents were safe. All he wanted to do, by making me an elf, was to give Santa Claus enough time to finish the inspections so that all the toys would be ready for the children on Christmas Eve."

"I was standing as I looked down at him and said, 'I'm sorry, Marcus. I've messed things up for you'."

"'You know Dillon, I might have to wait 300 years to get another chance to be one of Santa's helpers. But finding you and bringing you in from the cold was worth it. Come on, there are other jobs that we can learn, and I think it will be a lot of fun.'"

"I stayed for a long time in Santa village, and I sure did learn a lot of things about making toys. I also met a lot of Santa's elves. Time was different there, but the one thing I do know is that Santa was not late for Christmas because he took me with him to help deliver Christmas presents."

"No, I didn't get to crawl down any chimneys like he did, but I did get to go to one special house. The ride through the sky was like nothing I had ever experienced. Your grandmother and I had flown in an airplane only two months before, and it was nothing like that. But like an airplane, I could not feel the wind, and I could not feel the cold even though I knew we were outside. We were moving because I could see everything passing by far below us, but, they looked so close that I felt as if I could reach out and touch them."

"Santa looked huge in his red suit. He laughed all the time while he was sitting next to me, and his laugh drowned out the thunder that was all around us. We were flying through the sky with animals that did indeed look like reindeer. Suddenly we headed straight up, like we were trying to reach beyond the clouds, and before I knew it, we were under the moon, and above the clouds that were dark and stormy below us. Lightning shot from the clouds directly toward us, but it passed us by as if we were not even there. We were flying with such speed that I knew we must be traveling thousands of miles an hour."

"I looked over at Santa sitting beside me in the sleigh, not knowing who or what he was because I was so confused. I cannot remember all of that night. It was as if I was in some kind of a dream, and when I again looked at Santa he was not there. In his place was a little short man with pointed ears. Then another little man took his place, then another and another and all the little men were laughing. All the different little men had funny colorful clothing and little sharp ears. There was only one thing they had in common — they were all happy and laughing. The reindeer also looked as if they were laughing as they pulled the sled through the sky."

"I saw the lights of a farm in front of me and somehow I knew it was a special farm. Snow was flying through the air, but I could see colored lights hanging on the trees. I had seen them someplace before, but could not remember where. There was laughter and more laughter, and suddenly, the reindeer turned into the farm yard. I knew this place. I had been here before."

"The sled stopped, and the fat man in the red suit had replaced the funny little men. He was still laughing as the door of the farm house opened. Standing in the door was someone I knew, but could not remember from where. Then someone else stood in the doorway. It was my mother, but how did I know that? My grandfather was there too. It was as if I was looking at a life I had known before, but how was all this possible? I had never really known what Santa looked like because I had stopped believing in him when I was seven years old."

"The fat man was still laughing as he placed me on the porch. My mother, my father, and my grandparents could not believe what they were seeing. My parents had been rescued only a few minutes after I had gotten out of the car and headed toward the gas station. But I had not been found. My folks had spent two days in the hospital and were now at my grandparents' farm. There were still search crews out looking for me, but everyone was sure

I would not be found alive. Apparently, the star I had seen had pointed me in the right direction, but the station was too far away for me to make it on foot."

"'MERRY CHRISTMAS!' I heard the fat man say. 'I've brought you your Christmas present. My elves sure had lots to do to get ready for Christmas, and without Dillon we might not have made it.'"

"My father said that the man in the red suit turned away and laughed all the way back to his sled which quickly pulled away and disappeared into the snowy night. The last thing my parents heard was 'MERRY CHRISTMAS TO EVERYONE.'"

"The papers back home reported that a local boy had seen a star in the sky, and it had saved his life. They didn't want to tell all my story: that Mr. Marcus William Handfield, Jr, one of Santa Claus' elves, was the one who had found me. Nor did they want to say that it was Santa Claus who allowed me to stay at his workshop and learn about why we give presents at Christmas."

"When I asked about the star, Santa Claus said it was not him, but maybe it was his Boss because He had been known to help people believe."

"I'll be right back," I told my son. When I returned, I laid a small bag on the table in front of Andy. The bag had all sorts of colors on it. One second it looked blue, but if he moved his hand only slightly, it would turn red, or yellow, or green, or a hundred other different colors. After a while, when he looked at it, he couldn't be sure what color it was because it kept changing so fast. At the same time, he could see right through it as if it were some kind of crystal material, like clear ice.

"The night I left for home, Mr. Marcus gave me this small bag so I could remember him. But, right now, come on. Mom, Tiffany. Let's go get ourselves some ice cream."

After we got our ice cream, I went back into the living room, but, Andy wasn't there. I saw that the small bag was empty and found Andy outside in front of our house looking up into the sky. I didn't say anything as I stopped next to him.

"Dad, is that it? Is that the star?"

Looking up into the clear night sky, we saw what looked like a bright star, much larger than normal.

"You think it is showing someone the way?" Andy asked as he handed me a set of rubber ears that were pointed on one end, along with a small piece of paper. Looking at the paper, I saw it changing color as I held it in my hand. I did not have to read what was written on one side. I had read it every Christmas for the last twenty-five years.

"Thank you, Dillon, for the time we spent together. I made it."

Your friend,
Marcus William Handfield, Jr.

"Yes, I do son. Yes, I do," I said as I placed my arm around his shoulder. "God is always looking out for us even when we think He is not."

IT TAKES ONLY ONE HAND

George Madison was walking down the hall at his small high school during his third year and noticed a new student he had not seen previously. The boy was standing alone, and what caught George's attention was his clothing. It looked clean, but was tattered. He noticed the same young man again standing alone the following day as other students passed him by without saying anything.

During George's history class, he saw the boy sitting in the back of the classroom. As he walked by, he noticed the book on the boy's desk was <u>The Life of President Franklin D. Roosevelt</u>. George had always loved history, and since he was the kind of guy who tried to like everyone, he decided to meet this new student. As the boy was leaving class, George introduced himself.

"Hi, my name is George Madison. Nice to meet you." George held out his hand just as his father had taught him to do when meeting someone. Most of his friends thought it was corny to shake hands with other guys when they first met, but George didn't because his father had taught him that it was not only the right thing to do, it was the Christian thing to do.

"Recognizing that all men are creatures of God makes it easier to start a conversation with them and even share our faith when the opportunity presents itself. Don't go up and just start talking about how great God is. Shake the stranger's hand warmly and show them how great God is." His father's technique sure had helped him meet a lot of nice people and had given him a chance to show them that they were special. It had a way of making folks feel good about themselves, plus George liked letting someone know that they were special in the eyes of God.

There were a lot of young people in his church that were already good Christians, but George wanted to bring someone new along the road to faith. He felt in his heart that was what God wanted from him, and that was why George was the way he was.

As a junior in high school, George stood six feet tall, and weighed 185 pounds. His naturally fit body looked like an Olympic wrestler's. He was a grade A student in all his classes, and was the school's star football player.

George knew he was special in the eyes of God just as everyone was, but he thought God had something for him to do in his life, so he would never stop searching until he found out what that was.

The new boy looked up at George, then at the extended hand. He did not hold out his own. Was this big guy standing in front of him trying to make a fool out of him? He had already felt the sting of rejection from some of the other students at school, so he lowered his head and put his hands in his pockets. He could feel some of the students watching.

"You're not going to make me feel stupid. I've already had enough of that," George heard the boy say.

George was shocked. "I don't want to make you feel stupid or ashamed. I'm George, and if you need a friend, I'll be here." George said in a quiet voice just loud enough for the boy to hear. Turning, George left the classroom.

On the following Sunday morning, George drove his car to pick up two of his friends to give them a ride to church. They could have driven themselves, but they always liked to ride together, and each week they would take turns picking up the others. This Sunday it was George's turn to drive.

Making his way through town, George passed the town's one and only homeless shelter. As he glanced toward the building, he said to himself, "Jesus, there are people in this world who could sure use your help." What surprised him was that he saw the new boy in school coming out the door of the shelter. Continuing on his way to get his friends, George couldn't fully understand what he saw. He thought, "Why is the new guy at school coming out of there?"

The ride to church did not have George's full attention. "What's eating you?" Samuel Hampton asked George. "You haven't said four words this morning."

"Have any of you seen the new guy in school?" said George.

"Yeah, I saw him," said Bobby Jones. "Kind of odd. Doesn't talk to anyone, but I did see that jerk, Richard Thomas, and some of his friends giving him a hard time at school. I heard he lives downtown someplace. His name is Henry something."

"I've never heard someone having a last name of `something'," said Hank, the third friend George had picked up that morning. It brought a little laugh from Bobby, but for George, it brought back the image of Henry coming out of the shelter.

"Hey George, where are you going to go on Christmas vacation? Going back to you grandparents' place this year?"

"Actually, we're not going anywhere. My grandparents are coming here for Christmas. Dad and I put up the lights in early December. My grandpa always loves seeing the lights during the holidays."

During Sunday morning services, George looked over at his father and spoke softly, "Dad, how do we know when God has something He wants us to do, especially at this time of year?"

"If you think He has something special for you to do during this time, perhaps He has already shown you. Sometimes it is not easy for us to see the direction He wants us to go, but a little praying does not hurt."

Christmas was a wonderful time for George's family. It was the one time of year when they all got to celebrate together. George's sister and her family would be coming in from Washington State, his brother and his family from Texas, and his grandparents from Kansas. They would all spend a week celebrating this sacred season.

"I wonder what Henry will be doing for Christmas?" George thought.

After dropping off his friends after church, he again passed by the shelter, but he did not see Henry. He could not get the image out of his mind of Henry coming out of this refuge for the homeless. Pulling his car over to the side of the road, he stopped.

"Why am I doing this? It is none of my business why Henry went into the shelter. Maybe he was just going to visit someone who has gone through some hard times and wants to help them out." But George was not satisfied with his answer. Getting out of the car, he walked toward the front doors of the big building. He had never had any direct dealings with the organization, but his church did help support his city's homeless with food and clothing, and they sent money to help run the shelter. They even had a small food donation center inside their church. Families could pick up food items to help tide them over for a few days until they could get the help they needed.

As George entered the shelter, he had no idea what he would see. He knew he was being curious about something he should have already known more about.

What he saw were people. Not just people, but entire families — women with crying children, men having whispered conversations at tables, lone individuals looking as if there was no hope left in the world for them. George was hurt — not hurt in his body, but in his heart. He thought he knew about the homeless, but he now realized that he knew nothing at all. Each person had a unique story of how their lives had been turned upside down. Each had their own sorrow because life had thrown its worst at them. Some would overcome their adversities, but some would never get over the feeling that God didn't even know they existed, if they had ever thought about God at all. Some would never feel the handshake of another human being that was truly a friend when they were in need of one.

When George drove away, he was more confused than he had been before he saw Henry come out of the shelter. Sadness filled his mind, but he was not sure why. Was God telling him something, or was he just trying to tell himself that God was?

On Monday morning, as George parked his car in the school parking lot, he saw Richard Thomas and three of his friends talking to Henry. Henry had his hands up as if he was going to defend himself. Backing out of the parking space, George drove over to the group. Stopping next to them, he got out of his car.

"Good morning, Henry. Hi, Richard," George said, "Come on Henry, we are going to be late for class. Bye, Richard."

George started to walk away but stopped, turned around and said, "Come on Henry. You can talk to your friends later after school. We're going to be late."

Henry had no idea what was going on, but he did know that this big guy was giving him a way out of an uncomfortable situation with the four they were leaving behind. "Thanks," he said looking up at George. "Why did you do that?"

George looked over at Henry, "It seemed like a good thing to do at the time." Nothing else was said as the two departed. George knew that Richard and his friends would no longer bother Henry. He'd never had any real conversation with Richard. George had always been friendly to Richard, but his friendship had always been pushed away. He had made a pact with his two closest friends, Samuel and Bobby, who were also on the football team. They had decided between themselves that their actions needed to show other students what integrity was supposed to look like. That idea, however, had never rubbed off on Richard and his friends.

During lunch the next day, George saw Henry sitting alone in the school cafeteria, so he, Bobby, and Samuel sat down with him. George said, "Henry, what you going to do for Christmas?"

"I'm going to work at the homeless shelter," Henry said.

"What are you doing there?" asked Samuel, surprised.

Henry knew he was about to lose the three new friends he had just made. "I live there. My mother and I help in the kitchen, so we can have some place to stay until a day after Christmas. Our time will be up then, and uh, well, we'll be back on the streets again," he said looking down at the floor.

George was shocked. He could not believe what he had just heard. Now he knew why he had seen Henry come out of the shelter. "Back on the streets. What do you mean, 'back on the streets'?"

"Our time will be up, so we have to leave. We have been able to stay there longer than most because we work in the kitchen. After that, if we can find someplace close, maybe I can stay in school. I want to finish so that I can get a job and take care of my mother."

"I'm sorry, Henry. I'm sure something will work out," said Bobby.

"Me too," said Samuel.

Henry was surprised to hear what his new friends said after they heard that he and his mother would have to leave the shelter. Usually when people learned that he and his mother lived at such a place, they wanted nothing more to do with him. He expected it to be the same here, but after hearing their words, Henry had the feeling that it was not going to happen with these three.

"Henry, how does it happen that you live in a homeless shelter?" asked George. "I'm not trying to be nosy. I'm just trying to understand how something like that happened."

"My father died two years ago and we had no insurance or savings. We lost our home, and had to sell everything just to keep me in school. Mother worked hard to keep me in school because she wanted me to get an education and have a better life. After the company she worked for was sold, Mom lost her job, along with hundreds of other people. She found a new job here, but it doesn't start for another week. In the meantime, we have to have a place to live."

The school lunch bell rang and everyone headed out for their classes.

"I'll see you after school and give you a ride back to the shelter," said George. That was another surprise for Henry. No one had ever given him a ride, even if they were his friends. Most of his other friends didn't even have a car.

After school, George stopped outside the shelter and got out of the car with Henry.

"Where are you going?" asked Henry.

"I'm going inside with you. I want to see inside."

George didn't tell Henry he had seen part of the inside of the shelter before. He also did not want to explain to Henry that he was confused by what he saw. Going inside, Henry took George back to the kitchen and introduced him to his mother.

"Mom, this is George, one of my friends at school. He came by to see what the shelter looks like." Henry's mother was a small, kind, sweet woman. When she smiled at him, George could tell right away that he liked her.

"Hello, Mrs. Wilson. I'm glad to meet you." George held out his hand and when he took hers, he could see by the expression on her face that Mrs. Wilson was happy that her son had found a friend in his new school. Her hand was small compared to his, and George knew that he had just made another new friend.

That evening George was sitting with his father. "Dad, I was talking to Henry Wilson, a new guy at my school who lives at the shelter. I asked him what he and his mother were going to do for Christmas. He told me he was going to work at the shelter serving Christmas dinner to the homeless. I asked Mom if she thought it would be all right if Henry and his mother came and had Christmas dinner with our family. She said it would be fine. In fact, she thought it was a great idea. I told Henry, but he declined. After he saw all the people who needed help at the shelter, he wouldn't feel right sitting down at a big turkey dinner. Henry told me that there are so many people who are only going to get what others hand out to them in the way of charity, and it just wouldn't be right if he didn't try to help make a better Christmas for them."

"He sounds like a fine young man, and I'm thinking that he is doing the right thing for himself and his mother," said George's father.

Three days before Christmas, all of George's family gathered in the living room. Everyone was laughing at a joke one of the children had just told. Looking up, George's father asked why George was picking up all his presents from under the tree.

Looking at his mother and father, he said, "I'm sorry, but I can't be here for Christmas." Then he turned toward his grandparents. "I think I need to be standing next to Henry, a friend I met at school who is going to be serving food at the homeless shelter. I want to thank all of you for the presents you put under the tree for me, but I feel that they need to go somewhere else."

George saw that the children were devastated at what he just said. They had spent a long time finding just the right gift for their uncle. George sat down and faced his family. For the next twenty minutes he explained how he felt and what he had learned by being at the shelter over the last few days. He told them about the looks of hopelessness on the faces of so many people who knew there would be very little joy for them on Christmas. George told how Henry's family had kindly refused his offer to spend the holiday with them so that they could serve the homeless.

"When I first saw the shelter, I told God that there were people in our town that needed so much, and prayed that He would help them. What I later realized was that I was leaving it up to God to do the work. I was doing nothing while Henry, who was one of those having a hard time, was doing everything he could for those around him who were homeless just like he was. I have decided I want to help the less fortunate have a better Christmas. I feel in my heart that it is the right thing for me to do this year."

Turning to the children, George looked at them and said, "I know you bought my presents with money you earned working around the house, and I thank you so much. But I believe God wants your presents to go someplace else, a place where they are needed so much more than here. Will you please understand?"

Nine-year-old George, named after his uncle, got out of his chair and went to the Christmas tree and picked up a present that had his name on it. Walking over to George he handed it to his uncle. Then he went back, found two more and brought them to George as well.

"See, I can help too," he said. Then he stuck out his hand just as his uncle George had taught him to do. George knew what little George was trying to say. He was not meeting a new friend, but he was telling his Uncle George that he really wanted to help out also.

"I have a friend who does not have a father and is not going to get very much for Christmas," young George said. "And when I get back home, I'm going to give him something for Christmas."

"You know, I've got an idea," said George's father.

The following day George's father spoke with the city council and received enough money to purchase winter clothing from the thrift stores in their town and several other communities that did not have homeless shelters. It was a massive effort and once the word went out what George was doing, others wanted to help. Not only those in the town of Cotton Grove wanted to help, but several other communities wanted to help as well. Unlike the big cities where money and presents came in by the truck load, this outpouring of generosity came from individuals who often had very little themselves. It was a new beginning for George, his family, and the entire area.

On the night before Christmas, the people inside the homeless shelter heard singing outside their building. Opening the door, they saw a group of people singing Christmas carols. "Silent Night," "Away in a Manger," "Hark, the Herald Angels Sing," and many more. Behind them were two trucks and four police cars with their red and white flashing lights illuminating the darkness. Policemen also joined in the singing. In all, there were 60 people including small children with presents in their hands. The homeless people of the small community of Cotton Grove had a Christmas Eve they would always remember.

IN THE TOWN OF COTTON GROVE IT ONLY TOOK ONE HAND TO START A NEW BEGINING.

It has been written in this year of 2016 that the people of Vancouver, British Columbia, a long way from Cotton Grove, have come up with a new way for their homeless to find nighttime shelter. A local charity called Rain City Housing has created special benches that convert into temporary shelters. The back of the bench pulls up creating a shield for a homeless person to get out of the wind, rain, and snow. At night, they are easy to find because they have a message which glows in the dark and says, "THIS IS A SLEEP SPACE FOR YOU."

MY FRIEND SAM

Hi kids, I'm Joshua, and I would like to tell you a story about my friend Sam.

I suppose you might be wondering why I would want to tell you about my friend Sam, since I am a mouse and Sam is a puppy dog. Well, my story is interesting, because it's about how we both learned about God, Jesus, and Christmas.

I know it's going to be kind of hard for you to understand why a big little mouse and a small puppy dog would even care about Jesus or God, but we are part of God's creation. So it matters to us, and I hope Jesus matters to you. I also know that not many people like mice and everyone loves puppy dogs. Well, I'm going to forgive you for not loving me, but what I have learned is Jesus loves EVERYONE AND EVERYTHING, so that must mean He loves me too.

I can remember so clearly, how my life in Christ and Christmas started. (In case you didn't know, Christ is another name for Jesus). My story really started the day I told my family it was time for me to go out into the world and be a mouse on my own. I remember the day that I first spoke to my parents about leaving to find my own way.

"Mother. Father. I am old enough to go out into the big world and find my own place to live and start a family of my own."

"Joshua, you are much too small to be out in such a big world by yourself," my mother said, looking at me like I had lost my mind.

"Mother," my father said. "It had to happen someday, and Joshua is a big little mouse, so let him find out what is out there for him to see."

So, off I went, scurrying through the rocks, brush, and fallen trees looking for a place that would be just right for me to make a new home. I searched all day, but found nothing I liked. It was starting to get dark, and I knew I had to find someplace soon. Off in the distance, I could see a big barn on a small farm and knew that it would surely have a nice place for me to live. When I got to the barn, I found that too many mice were already living there.

"You can't stay here," an old mouse told me. "There is no room for you. You can spend the night, but tomorrow you will have to find another place to live."

"That's okay. I'll find another place tomorrow. Maybe I can go and live at the farmer's house."

"I wouldn't do that either. There is a big cat named Crispy living there, and he doesn't like it when we go into the house. There hasn't been a mouse in that farmhouse for years."

I did not sleep well that night, because I was wondering where I would be able to find myself a home. I decided that since a mouse had not lived in the farmhouse for so long, maybe Crispy had forgotten about us.

The next morning, I made my way to the farmhouse. Finding a hole going under the house, I carefully entered and came out beneath the floor in a big wide open area. There was no Crispy. It was nice and warm, so I decided that I would make my new home right there. But, I would keep my eye out for Crispy, the farmer's cat.

In and out of the hole I went, bringing in grass and leaves until I had made myself a nice nest. Now, it was time for me to go exploring the farmhouse. I found lots of old holes in the walls, and spent days going into every one of them. There was a tiny hole that I could not go through, but I could see inside the house. Since I could not see very well, I decided to make the hole just a little bigger. I must have forgotten myself, because I made the hole so big that I could go right through it if I wanted.

The following day, I crawled through the hole and hid under a big box. I could see Crispy on the other side of the room, and I could also see a little boy and girl along with their mother and father. The little boy and girl were crying as they knelt down next to Crispy. Oh! It was so sad. I knew what had happened. Crispy was gone, and there would be no more cat in the farmhouse.

Watching the family, I saw them join hands and say, "The Lord is my shepherd," followed by a bunch of other words I could not understand. Then the father picked up Crispy and carried him outside.

I ran through the walls and out the hole under the house. I wanted to see what the father was going to do with poor Crispy. I watched as he dug a hole in the ground and put Crispy into it. The boy and girl were still crying, and I really did feel bad for them. Crispy was indeed gone.

I saw the mother, father and the two children again holding hands for a long time. The father said, "Let us pray one more time for Crispy." Then he said a bunch of words for Crispy.

Now, the farmhouse was all mine. I didn't have to worry about Crispy finding me and having me for lunch or supper. But I still felt bad for him because he had never come under the house to bother me. I couldn't understand what all the fuss was about from the other mice in the barn. However, I was not going to tell them that Crispy no longer lived in the house. If I did, all of them would want to come and live with me.

Every morning, I did what big little mice were supposed to do. When inside the farmhouse, I stayed under a large chest and out of sight. Every evening, I watched as the family held hands and said some words before they ate. After everyone was gone, I would run out from my hiding place to where the children sat to find food scraps they had dropped onto the floor.

Collecting all of the crumbs, I took them back inside the wall and saved them for later. Every time the family ate, they would talk about someone they called Jesus. They did it so much that I even learned a few of their words. They also talked about prayer, God our Lord, and always about Jesus at every meal. I learned that the little girl was called Sally and the little boy was called Mickey.

Every week on a day the family called Sunday, they left, and I had the farmhouse all to myself. I got to play around in all the rooms until they came home. I sure did like that time alone knowing the place was all mine. Then one day, they came back early while I was upstairs in little Sally's room. The father put Sally into bed, and I had to hide under it all day because her mother did not leave Sally's side. I found out that Sally was sick, and her mother prayed many times for her that day. I was really surprised when Sally prayed before she went to sleep even though she was sick. I couldn't hear all her prayer, but I did hear, "Dear Jesus, we love you."

It took me a long time to learn enough of what they were saying to understand that the man they called Jesus must have been a kind person. Listening to them every day made me wonder about a lot of things. I was just a big little mouse, but could there be a place up there in Heaven even for me?

I stayed under the house that first summer. Then it started getting cold outside, and it began to snow. In spite of the cold, it was so pretty with everything so white, and I did not worry because I had the whole warm farmhouse to myself. I was hiding under the couch one day when the father brought in a small tree and put it in the big room. I sure was curious when I saw him put all kinds of colored lights on the tree. Then the father watched as the mother and children put pretty things all over it.

Finally, the father turned on the lights and the tree was just beautiful. Over the next few weeks, a few pretty boxes they called presents were placed under the tree. Then one night lots of presents, were placed under it. I did not get to see who put them there, because I was asleep, but the next morning Sally and Mickey blamed it on someone named Santa Claus. I got to watch as the family opened all the presents.

I really had to wonder what the big deal was about Christmas. There was a lot of laughing and hugging after everyone said, "Merry Christmas." Then, the whole family did something very funny. Everyone sat on the floor in a circle and held hands. The father gave a short prayer and started talking about what Christmas was really about.

They were not speaking very loudly, and I really did want to hear, so I left my hiding place and raced across the room to get closer. Just as I ducked behind a cabinet, I heard Sally say, "Daddy, you promised."

"After we finish our discussion about the birth of Christ," the father told Sally.

The family talked about when Jesus was born and what it meant to the world. I was really interested because I knew the family was talking about me too, since I was one of God's creatures. After the family stood up and had one last prayer, the father went into the other room.

It was on that Christmas day that disaster struck my happy home. When the father came back into the big room, he carried a box for the children. The box kept moving around. There had been so much laughing and hugging that I was even happy myself, but when a big giant dog came out of that box, I was really scared. How was I going to get back across the room with that big thing running all over the place?

I watched the dog. It was the first one I had ever seen, but I had heard all about them. It was huge. A monster! The dog was sniffing everything in the room, and then suddenly it was right there standing in front of me. I was frozen like the popsicles I saw the kids eating during the summer. Suddenly a big wet nose pushed right up against me. I had my eyes closed, but I could hear it take a big sniff of me. Then Mickey started calling, "Here Sam. Here Sam. Oh Dad! We love our new puppy."

The monster turned and ran over to Mickey and Sally. While everyone had their eyes and hands on that huge dog, I ran across the room and back toward my hole. I saw the monster turn its head and look at me just as I went under the box.

I stayed under the house and out of sight for a long time. Then one Sunday, while the family was gone, I went through the hole to see if the kids had left any food on the floor. I found nothing. That big monster had eaten every tiny little scrap. I was really upset, but then I remembered one of the things I had heard the family talking about. "Forgive us our trespasses as we forgive those who trespass against us." Okay, it took me a while to understand what that meant. Even then, it was only after a couple of lessons from the father explaining it to Sally and Mickey that I finally got it. Alright, I am going to forgive that big monster of a dog, but next time I'll come early and find the food before he eats it all up.

I went through my hole the next morning, and then ran along the wall of the kitchen. I stopped beside the kitchen cabinets and started making a hole as fast as I could so I could get under them. I almost had it done when something behind me said. "Hi, what are you doing?" I froze. What else could I do? I turned around very slowly. There it was. That monster dog was standing over me.

The monster's head was close, so close I could have reached out and touched it. In the monster's head were two big, brown eyes. His huge tongue was hanging out as if it were ready to lap me up at any second. His ears were so long, they almost touched the floor. I was finished! I was going to be his morning snack. But the monster just stood there looking at me. Disaster was about to strike, and I would be a goner like Crispy, except I would have no one to say a prayer over me.

"What are you doing?" the dog said in a low deep voice.

It took a little time for me to say anything. "Making a hole," I told the monster.

"Why?"

"Because you took all the food, and I was going to come early this morning and get some to hide in the hole before you got it."

"Why?"

"Look here, dog. You already have me, so I might just as well be honest and brave before you eat me."

"I'm not going to eat you. I'm not hungry."

"You're not?"

"Of course not. You are the only one I know around here."

"Look here, monster dog, you have Sally and Mickey. There are your friends."

"Yes, that is true, but I can't talk to them."

"Monster dog, my name is Joshua. What is your name?"

"The children said I am a Sam, but my real name is Basset Hound. And I'm not a monster. I'm just a puppy."

"Okay, to make it easy, I'll call you Sam also. Sam, I'll make you a deal. You can have all the big pieces the kids drop on the floor, and I'll take the small ones. Okay?"

"No,"

"No? What do you mean, NO? It sure sounds like a good deal to me."

Sam looked down at me with big sad eyes and then said, "Henry, you can have all the scraps the kids drop. I've got food. You can even have some of mine, if you like. Look over there in that big bowl. I don't think you would eat too much, and there is enough for both of us."

Going over to the bowl, I saw food above the rim of the bowl.

"Sam, I might be a big little mouse, but there is no way I'm getting up there. It's just too tall."

Sam picked me up in his mouth and very gently dropped me into the bowl.

"Sam, this stuff is not bad. Are you sure you don't mind sharing a little with me?"

"No, you go right ahead. You just come back and talk to me once in a while."

It was on that very day that Sam became my friend. He was not the disaster I thought he was going to be. Not only did I come back once in a while to talk to Sam, I came back every day. I didn't want to miss what the father was going to say about Jesus and God. I wasn't sure why, but I thought there might be something more for me to learn.

Every day I listened to what the children's father had to say while Sam mostly slept. He just wasn't interested in hearing about Jesus or God. To him, it just wasn't anything for him to be concerned about.

Then Christmas arrived, and I knew it was going to be "yum-yum" time. After what I had learned last year, there would be people stopping by with lots of kids and you know what that means — big hunks of sweet stuff falling on the floor.

The father of the family again brought in a small tree and put lights on it. Sam and I were watching, when Sally yelled, "I see a mouse. Dad, I see a mouse!" I had not been watching for the kids, and when Sally came into the big room, she saw me. Not knowing what to do, I jumped right onto Sam's neck.

"Quick, get behind my ear," Sam told me, and I did just what he said for me to do. Then, I snuggled down under his long ear. Ooh, my, it was nice and warm!

"Where did you see the mouse?" Sally's father asked.

"Over by Sam. Sam was looking right at the mouse."

Walking over next to Sam, Sally's father looked around. "I don't any mouse here. If there had been one here, Sam would have let us know by barking at it."

"He wouldn't have killed it?" asked Mickey.

"No, I don't think Sam could kill anything," answered Mickey's father. Then the children's father went back to the tree. I was safe under Sam's ear, and I hoped I would not let Sally see me again.

"What's he doing?" asked Sam.

"He's putting up the Christmas tree," I answered.

"Now, why would he put a tree inside the big room?" Sam wanted to know.

"They are going to have Christmas. It is the time of Jesus' birth, and they are going to celebrate that He came into the world to save them."

"Save them from what? I don't see anything that would harm them. If it were here, I would chase it right out of the house."

"Okay, I guess I am going to have to get you caught up on what you have been missing out on. Jesus was born over 2016 years ago."

"No one can live that long," Sam said.

"No, no, no! That was when He died. He died to save everyone's souls, maybe even yours and mine. They remember His birth by celebrating it on Christmas Day. You will see lots of people come to the house and bring presents. That is their way of sharing with other people and saying they remember Him in their hearts, too. I'll bet the kids will even have something for you, Sam."

"Something for me! Why?"

"It is their way of showing you that they love you. It is what Jesus did a long time ago. He shared the words of God with the people and taught them how God wanted them to live and care for one another. You see that big book over there, the one the children's father always reads from? Well, those are all the stories about Jesus. When I first came into the big room, I was going to chew holes into it. But after I found out what it said, I knew I couldn't do it. I sure wish I could read."

"Why?" asked Sam.

"Well, if you had been listening, and I mean really listening, then you would have understood what Jesus did for the world. He died for all the sins of the people and gave them a way to sit next to him in Heaven. Christmas is only one of the times the world says `Thank you, Jesus.' Of course lots of people remember him every day, but Christmas is a special day of remembering when he was born."

"Well," said Sam. "I think I should be listening a little more closely to what the children's father says to see if I can learn something. Then I can tell it to you, and…"

"There it is! There's the mouse!" screamed Sally. "I saw it over by Sam. Look it's climbing onto his neck. Daddy look at it. The mouse went behind Sam's ear."

I was a goner. Sam and I were not watching the kids, and I was seen again. But as Sally's father came over to Sam, the dog did not let the father get too close before he got up and walked into the other room.

"Here Sam," the father said, but Sam did not stop. Once in the other room and out of sight of the father, I jumped out from behind Sam's ear and ran for my hole. Sam turned around and went back into the big room and right up to the children's father.

After checking Sam and finding nothing, the father told Sally she must have been seeing something other than a mouse. After that day, I not only got to ride behind Sam's ear, I got to stay with him and get really close to the father to hear everything he told the children about Jesus.

We learned more about love and forgiveness. We learned how people were supposed to live their lives in His name. We also learned more about sharing and what Christmas was all about.

I know, I'm just a big little mouse, and Christmas is really not about me or Sam. It is about you and your walk with Christ and how you remember His birth, His life, and His death at this special time of year.

Me, I love Christmas and all the people who come to visit. I love the Christmas tree the children's father puts in the big room every year. With all the lights and decorations. It is just beautiful. I love the sweet YUM-YUMS the children drop on the floor, and Sam and I have learned a lot about God's son.

There is something else you need to know. Sam got a great big bone this Christmas, and me, well, Sally came up to Sam, lifted his ear, and put a big piece of cheese under it. Now, who do you think that was for?

A WHISPER IN THE WIND

"Dad, tell us a Christmas story," my three children said as we finished putting up the tree. "Please tell us again how you found out Santa Claus was real," they all said at once. They must have all been thinking the same thing.

I was standing at the time, looking down at my wife, Margaret, and my children who were all sitting on the floor. I couldn't help but be a very proud father. Our tree was small, not much bigger than my oldest ten-year-old son Billy, but the love our family had in putting up the tree together was as big as anything in the world.

Margaret looked up and smiled. She had heard the same story many times during her life. I had repeated it for the last ten years since Billy's first Christmas, yet she never seemed to tire of hearing it again. She was nodding her head in an affirmative way as she looked up at me. I sat down on the floor, took a deep breath, and began.

"Okay, I'll tell it one more time. But this will be the last time." However, I knew that when Christmas came around next year, I would again be telling this same story to our children.

I started the story by lowering my voice, "It was a dark night, and Santa saw the clouds swirling all around him as he drove his reindeer through the darkness." *I raised my voice back to normal.* "He surely didn't want to be late delivering his presents across the world. But the wind was constantly changing from one direction to another as if it was trying to blow him off the course he must take in order to be at the right place at the right time on Christmas Eve. He had only delivered half of his presents when a big gust of wind slammed into the side of his sled."

"'Hold on, fellows!' Santa hollered to the nine reindeer pulling the sled. 'It sure is a bumpy ride tonight. Rudolph, you keep your nose shinning bright because we still have a lot of presents to deliver. Wouldn't want to miss any of the children,' Santa Claus said, as the wind became stronger."

"Father, there are only eight reindeer," said my six-year-old daughter, Sandy.

"Well," I said, looking down at her large green eyes. "Santa had to add Rudolph to lead the others because it was so dark and stormy. So, on that night before Christmas, he was using nine reindeer instead of eight."

"Oh....," Sandy whispered in her small voice, her eyes getting larger as she visualized Rudolph leading Santa's reindeer through a dark and stormy night.

"At the very moment Santa told Rudolph to keep his nose shinning bright, a little compartment door in the sled blew open and his list of all good children in the world was suddenly flying along with the wind. As the list lifted into the air, it separated into thousands of individual pages sending them in all directions.

"'Circle about so that we can catch all those pages,' Santa told his reindeer."

"In less than a minute, Santa had collected all the sheets of paper that held the names of the children who were to receive presents that Christmas Eve." *I lowered my voice a little and looked down at my children.*

"Starting out again, Santa heard something whispering in the wind." *I raised my voice back up to its normal tone.*

"It was not coming from the front. 'It must be coming from behind me,' Santa thought as he looked behind him and heard it again."

"'Santa where are you? Where are you, Santa?'"

"He could hear it clearly. The voices of three children were suddenly all around him, but he was sure he had not missed a single child on the list. 'What is going on?' Santa wondered."

"'It must be only the wind whispering to the clouds. Sometimes the wind will move through the trees singing to anyone who will listen, and I'm sure that is what I must have heard. Yes, the wind is racing through the clouds so swiftly, that I only think I hear three children asking me to come back and deliver their presents,' he said to his reindeer."

"The wind blew stronger, but Santa did not allow it to delay him any longer. On he went, flying from house to house until he had completed his delivery of all the presents. 'Onward,' he said to his reindeer. 'We have to be home before the sun comes up.'"

"Santa's sled flew through the night sky, and he made it home long before the sun came up above the ice and snowy mountains that protected Santa's village. 'It was a wonderful trip,' he told all the reindeer, but as he looked into the back of his sleigh, he saw that three presents had fallen onto the floor of the sled."

"'How could that have happened? I have missed three children at Christmas. This has never happened before. What am I going to do? I must check my list and somehow get the three presents to the children,' he told the reindeer surrounding him."

"Going through the pages of names, Santa was surprised when he found one page missing. 'How could I have missed a page? It was the storm. The wind must have taken part of my list. Now, I will not be able to deliver presents to the three children I missed.'"

"It was the night before Christmas, and Santa was not very happy with himself. There would be three children who would no longer believe in him because he had failed as Santa Claus. 'I must talk to the elves. Maybe they will have an idea of what I should do.'"

"Getting all his elves together, Santa told them how the storm had taken away one page of the children's list, and he now had three presents he could not deliver."

"'Santa, I must confess to you that I put an extra present into the sled,' said Theo, one of Santa's elves."

"'I also put an extra present in the sled,' said Basil, another one of Santa's helpers."

"'It was I, who put an extra present into the sled,' said a small voice behind Theo. Persil, being the smallest elf Santa had, was often out of sight among the other elves. Theo reached down, picked up Persil and placed him on his shoulder so that Santa could see who was speaking."

"'So, that is the reason we have three extra presents. I am happy that I did not miss any of the children,' Santa told all his elves. 'But why did each of you put one extra present into the sled?'"

"'Because it was the right thing to do,' all three elves said at the same time."

"For Santa, it was a puzzling thing for his elves to do. Never before had any extra presents been placed into his sled. But he had also never before heard the wind whispering to him with the voices of children."

"Santa went back to his reindeer. He had to find the three children and deliver their presents to them. But, before he departed, two of his oldest elves, Emil and Arver, stopped by his side and said, 'I think you are going to need these, Santa,' and handed him two more presents. Five presents for five very good children who were not on his list. He was sure of it." *I raised my voice, moved one hand, and then the other into the air.*

"'Dasher, Dancer, Prancer and Vixen, Comet, Cupid, Donner and Blitzen. Are you ready to take one more flight tonight?" *I dropped my hands, and returned my voice to normal.* "Rudolph, you shall lead again because the storm is still out there, and we will need your bright shiny nose to show us the way. We must return to where I heard the whisper in the wind. We must find out what else it has to tell us this Christmas Eve, but we must hurry because the light of day will soon be here.'"

"Off Santa flew with only five presents in his sled, and it wasn't long before he could again hear the voices whispering to him." *I again lowered my voice and placed my hand up next to my face.*

"'Santa, where are you? Where are you, Santa?'"

Looking down at my children, I waited a few seconds before I continued with their favorite Christmas story.

"Santa followed the whispering voices to a small village high in the mountains. The cold wind blew through the valley where the voices were the strongest. Landing outside a small wooden house, Santa listened to the wind as it told him what it heard from inside the house the night before. Words that came from inside the house — 'I tell you there is no such thing as a Santa Claus — never has been, now or ever. I grew up without Christmas and so will you three. We don't need to have Christmas here in this house!'"

"'But, Mother, all the kids at school tell us that he is real. All you have to do is believe. None of them have seen him, but he comes to their house every year. Christmas is the time to celebrate the birth of Christ. All we have to do is believe in Him, even though we can't see Him. Isn't it the same with Santa Claus?'"

"'I'm sorry, but Christmas if for fools. There is no Santa Claus. A God there is. People have written about Him for over two thousand years. We hear every year about how they have found something new that proves the Bible stories are true, and that He is real. But, has anyone ever found anything that proves Santa Claus is real? The answer is no, and they never will because Santa Claus is just a fairy tale for children,' the mother emphasized."

"'So, that is why the wind is whispering to me on this Christmas Eve,' thought Santa Claus. 'It is telling me that three children who should have received presents will not because their mother does not believe in me. I do not have a way of showing her that I am truly here, but I must somehow get the children's presents to them,' Santa said."

"Then he heard voices behind him that were not whisperings in the wind."

"'Why don't you just put them on the step in front of the door this year since there is no Christmas tree?' asked Theo, as he popped his head up in the back of the sled."

"'Yes, put them by the door,' said Emil, Arver, Basil and Persil as they also raised their heads out from under the bags that once held all of Santa's presents."

"'What are you elves doing here?' asked Santa."

"'We just wanted to help, and it was the right thing to do,' the five elves again said all together."

"Then, Emil and Arver brought a fully decorated Christmas tree out of the sled. 'Or we could just leave this,' they said as they set it down on top of the snow."

"Santa Claus fully understood what the five elves meant by, `it was the right thing to do.'"

"'Okay, let's get to work,' Santa told his helpers. 'We do not have long before the morning sun will be above the horizon, and we must be home when that happens.'"

"By the time the sun reached the horizon, Santa and his elves were sitting back in Santa's Village, watching the morning sun as it rose over the icy mountains." *I raised my voice.*

"'Mama, Mama, Mama. Look out in front of the house,' the three children yelled as they opened the door and looked out at the snow."

"Their mother, Silvia, looked out the window and saw a sparkling Christmas tree shining in the morning sun with five presents underneath."

"Dad, Silvia is the name of one of our grandmas," Sandy said so low that I could just barely hear the excitement in her voice.

"Stepping out into the snow, the family made their way to the tree. The children's mother was shocked at what she saw. There were prints of very small feet going all the way around the tree. Also, there were signs of a sled and the tracks of animals."

"Dad, they were reindeer. Even I know that," said my five-year-old very loudly as she raised her hands high above her head.

I looked down at Shirley and smiled. Then I placed my finger over my lips as if to show her that we were hiding a secret. Shirley lowered her hands, covered her mouth, and looked up at me with beautiful blue eyes. She knew that the secret of her grandma and the reindeer must remain within our family. I looked at my three children and continued, glancing at my wife. I saw a smile on her face.

"The tracks the woman was looking at did not come from any place that she could see, nor did the tracks go anywhere. But, there was a long line of tracks indicating very clearly where the animals and a sled had been on top of the snow. They just started and stopped right there."

"There was a card on the tree, and the children's mother reached out to lift it off. Opening the card, the mother read: 'I'm so sorry that I was not allowed to be there for you when you were a child. Please don't deny your children the wonderful experience of honoring the birth of Christ by sharing in this very special celebration. MERRY CHRISTMAS.'"

"She looked very closely at the signature on the card. She saw two words, 'Santa Claus.'"

"On each of the presents was the name of one of her children. But there were still two more presents, and to her surprise, on the fourth present was the name Scout, the children's father. On the fifth present was her name."

"Slowly she followed her family back into the house. She could not understand how the people in the village could have put a Christmas tree in their yard without leaving any tracks in the snow. There should have been tracks coming from and going back to the village."

"Once inside, she sat down on the sofa and watched her children open their gifts. What else could she do? Someone had taken the time to try and fool her family, but she could not figure out how they had done it."

"Then her daughter, Emily, came over to her carrying her gift and said, 'Look, Mama, it is the new hat I saw in the store last spring — the one I asked you if I could have. You said no because we didn't have the money. But, you knew Santa was going to bring it to me for Christmas, didn't you?'"

"Her son, Mark, was next. 'Look, Mama! Santa Claus brought me a new pair of ice skates. Now, I can skate with the other boys this winter!'"

"Olivia's youngest daughter stood and looked at the doll she had in her hands for several minutes with tears running down her face before she wrapped her arms around it and hugged it to her body. Then she said, 'Thank you, Santa.'"

"'Honey, how did you know to give me this gift?' the children's father asked. 'And why did you change your mind about Christmas?'"

"Looking up, Silvia seemed dazed as she looked at a tool in her husband's hand — the one she had heard he needed almost two years before but could not afford to buy."

"Her own present was small. Much smaller than any of her children's or their father's. Reaching out, Silvia put her hand on the gift, but could not make herself open it. She was completely confused about what had just happened on that cold Christmas morning."

"Going back to the window, she looked out, but saw nothing. There was no shining tree. Running out the door, she stopped where the tree should have been. There was no tree, no sled, nor small footprints. There was no sign of tracks where animals had stood. Everything was as it had been when they had all gone to bed on Christmas Eve."

"'What did you get from Santa, Mama?' asked her youngest daughter who was still hugging her new doll."

"Silvia lowered her head and looked down at her daughter. 'What have I done for so many years?' she thought. 'Could it be true? Could there truly be a Santa Claus. Would the true God have made such a person to teach us the way of sharing on the day of His son's birth?'"

"'No, it has to be just a fairy tale. But, could God have inspired some individuals to invent stories as a way to teach us about forgiveness, love, sharing, and all the other things we should do to be more like His son?

Could He have encouraged the Christmas traditions to inspire us to live in love? Oh, I am so confused!'"

"Looking at her mother standing by the window staring out at the snow, eight- year-old Kathy saw that her mother was crying. 'Mother must be hurting really bad inside,' she thought."

"Yes, Silvia was confused because she believed in Jesus, and she knew that Christmas was to honor His birth. But, if Santa was just a fairy tale, where had these presents come from? Could it be that there were other ways that God speaks to the world that are not so apparent? She knew that Santa Claus had nothing to do with the birth of Christ in scriptures, but she now felt that maybe God was speaking to mankind through lessons that Santa could teach us. Santa Claus was beginning to feel real in Silvia's heart. For the first time, she was able to see that Christmas could be the time God tried to bring true goodness out in others."

"Dad, you forgot to tell us what was in the present," Shirley said, again raising her hands up into the air, but this time she had excitement on her face because she was sure he had forgotten the best part of the story.

"Well, Silvia always wanted a black and white pony like the one she saw on the neighbor's next door farm, but her father could not afford to buy it for her, so she never got her pony."

Reaching out, Margaret handed me a small object that just fit into my hand. Opening my hand, I showed my children a small wood carving, "Your mother's great-grandmother, Silvia, always loved her present from Santa Claus, and it has been passed down to each generation until it was given to your mother. Someday, it will go to one of you to remind us that Jesus was truly here on this Earth, and that Santa Claus is one of the ways God teaches us to show our love to one another."

"Get the magnifying glass," said Billy. "I want to see it."

Margaret already had the magnifying glass in her hand because, like every Christmas, all three of the children wanted to see the tiny, tiny, inscription on the belly of the small black and white wooden horse which read: "Made by Emil for Santa Claus and Silvia."

A CHRISTMAS AT SEA

Todd Billingham and his three children left Fort Myers, Florida early on December 24th on the sailboat Dolphin for a sail along the coast to visit their grandparents at Stock Island, Key West, Florida. Mrs. Billingham was already at her parents' home waiting for Todd and their children to arrive later that day. For the last two days, she and Grandma had been making Christmas cookies, putting decorations on the tree, wrapping presents, and getting everything ready for the holidays. On Christmas Eve, the entire family would attend evening church services to thank the Lord for the wonderful birth of Christ.

Her kids, 19-year-old Thomas, 14-year-old Billy, and nine-year-old daughter Jacklyn, were all excellent sailors. They had learned to sail from their father who took them out on the Gulf of Mexico regularly. On the day before, the weather was wonderful, and all the reports said it would remain calm out on the open water.

The family had made the one day trip many times to see their grandparents at Christmas. On this trip, they left early so they could take their time and do a little fishing along the way. The sailing was smooth with a light wind from the east. Heading west, they searched for a good fishing area.

Three hours out of Fort Myers they reached their favorite place to fish above several old shipwrecks. Then

Todd started feeling a sharp pain in his side. "Kids, I'm going down below to rest for a few minutes. Thomas, make sure all of you keep your life vests on. I'll be back up in a little while."

Billy went down into the cabin with his father, "Are you going to be okay, Dad?" he asked.

"Yes, I'm sure I'll be fine. I'll just rest here for a few minutes. You go back topside and help you brother," Todd told his youngest son.

An hour later, Todd had not returned, and Thomas saw that the sky had darkened and the wind was becoming stronger.

"Jacklyn, go down and see what is keeping Dad, will you?"

A few minutes later, Jacklyn came hurrying back. "I can't wake Daddy. He won't open his eyes."

After Todd felt the pain in his side, he found that lying down did little to help. He tried to stand, but became so sick that he fell back onto the bunk and promptly closed his eyes to the world. Thomas told Billy to take over the wheel, then rushed down to check on his father, but he was not able to wake his father either.

The wind continued to became stronger. Thomas tried calling in an emergency as the boat blew further out to sea, however, he could get no response over the radio. Realizing they were in real trouble, he tried to remember everything his father had told him about an emergency situation on the open sea. The first thing he did was make sure everyone had their life jackets on correctly. Their father would not allow anyone on the sailboat to be without one, and that it fit properly. "Secure all the hatches and get everything tied down to keep things from being washed overboard," he knew his father would say. He also checked the small lifeboat to make sure everything was as it should be.

With their father severely ill and unable to help, Thomas had difficulty keeping the boat heading back toward land. As the wind became stronger, Billy and Jacklyn did what they could to help Thomas while continuing to check on their father. The sea became rougher, and suddenly a huge wave swept over the craft, pouring through the cabin door which Jacklyn had not properly closed. It was not long before the small engine Thomas was using to help them stay on course suddenly stopped — flooded by the incoming water. Thomas would have to get them home with what he had learned from his father.

Several hours later, Thomas knew the sailboat was way off course, but all he could do was try to keep heading toward land. Closing his eyes, he prayed, "Our Lord Jesus, we are in a bad situation here. Give me strength and enough wisdom to bring us through this, and please look after my dad. You know I cannot do it alone, so I'm asking for your help. I ask that you guide my heart and hands to bring my family to safety. I would really appreciate the help, because we could sure use it."

Billy tried the radio again but could only get static, and told his brother that the radio was not working at all.

By this time, Thomas had no idea where they were. As the day wore on, time seemed to speed up, it was getting dark, and it was the night before Christmas.

— — —

Flying high above the clouds, a spark of light streaked across the sky.

"Rudolph," Santa hollered. "It is going to be another bad one this Christmas Eve trying to cross these big waters so high up. You had better drop down lower to see if we can find smoother air." Leading the other reindeer, Rudolph the Red-Nosed Reindeer shot straight down out of the sky.

"Not too fast, Rudolph. We don't want to hit the water," Santa yelled. Santa imagined that inside Rudolph's mind, there must be a smile, because he loved to go straight down and level out just above the surface of the water. Suddenly Rudolph's nose began to shine like a bright, red star, then he turned to the west.

"Rudolph, you're going the wrong way. You have traveled this route hundreds of times. Why would you make a mistake now?" Santa Claus hollered. However, Rudolph did not change course and acted like he had not heard Santa at all.

— — —

Suddenly another huge wave rose up in front of the sailboat, and there was a tremendous crash as the wall of water swept onto the deck. The sailboat was suddenly pushed over on its side and the rigging supporting the mast snapped. When the sailboat had righted itself, Thomas heard the mast crash onto the deck behind him. Realizing he no longer had any control, he again said a little prayer as the sailboat was pushed further west, out into the Gulf of Mexico.

"Jesus, we need a help!" Then Thomas said the Lord's Prayer, "Our Father who art in heaven......"

Down below deck, Billy tried to hold onto both Jacklyn and his father, but his sister slipped from his fingers. With the sailboat half full of water, Jacklyn struggled toward the cabin's open doorway just as another wall of water entered the lower deck. The incoming water opened an upper cabinet door allowing a box of canned fruit to tumble out, striking Jacklyn on her left shoulder. Even with her life jacket on, she was forced under the rushing water. As the water departed back out the cabin door, it carried Jacklyn along with it, spilled her onto the deck, then over the side of the boat. Then Jacklyn found herself in the open sea.

– – –

Santa saw a small sailboat in the extremely rough waters below and understood why Rudolph had made such a drastic change in their course. Off in the distance, Santa could also see a large aircraft carrier with its long flat runway filled with airplanes shining in the darkness, and he realized that the huge ship would never be able to spot the small sailboat so far away.

"It is the Billingham family in the sailboat Dolphin on their way to the children's grandparents for Christmas. They are such good children. I have only a few presents for them this year because they asked for little other than being with their family at Christmas," thought Santa Claus as he watched a wall of water rush over the sailboat. Then he saw a small girl tumble over the side. Within seconds she was floating in the open water all alone. "It is little Jacklyn Billingham, and she has been washed into the sea," Santa yelled. "Rudolph, drop us down to the water quickly!"

– – –

The Navy ship's helmsman saw a flash of bright red light shoot across the aircraft carrier's bow. Not knowing what it was, he pressed the alarm button. Instantly the huge ship came alive with men heading to their assigned stations. Pilots headed towards their aircraft, and crew members made ready for the aircraft to launch. The flash of red light crossed the bow again just as the captain reached the helmsman on the bridge.

"Sir, it did not come up on radar. There it is again, Sir."

"Yes, I see it. Get some pilots in the air immediately," the Captain directed the staff that had now filled the ship's control room. Within one minute, three

F/A-18E Super Hornet aircraft were in the air. Making a circle, they followed the red light as it again crossed directly over the ship. The light slowed almost to a stop above the Carrier as one of the Super Hornets flew by. The light stayed over the huge ship for a full 10 seconds before it again shot into the air. Directly behind the departing flash of light came the other two Super Hornets.

"You are not going to believe what we're seeing," came a voice over the ship's radio. "Can anyone else see what I'm seeing?"

"Yes, I see it, but I'm not going to tell anyone what it is," came the voice of another pilot.

"I'm sure going to tell my children what I saw today," the Captain heard the third pilot say. "This surely can't be designated top secret. Everyone already knows about him."

Suddenly the light moved like a speeding bullet through the air leaving the Super Hornets behind.

"He's gone, Captain. We just can't keep up with him. Those reindeer sure can fly!" came the voice of one of the pilots.

"Reindeer? And what do you mean, 'everyone knows about him?'" the Captain said into the ship's radio microphone. Before the Captain had received an answer from the pilots, he spoke again. "See what security found when the light stopped over the ship."

– – –

Billy continued to try and wake his father, but all he could do was keep his father's head above the rising water. Thomas, no longer able to control the sailboat, jumped down into the half-flooded cabin to help Billy get their father up onto the deck and into a lifeboat. It was a struggle to pull their dad up the stairs with the water constantly rushing in and out the cabin door.

"Where's Jacklyn?" Thomas yelled to Billy, as a rush of water slammed him in the back.

"The water took her up on the deck," Billy hollered back.

"I didn't see her up there. We've got to find her. Hurry, we have to get her and Dad into the lifeboat!"

— — —

A voice came over the control room radio. "Captain, you're not going to believe what we found on deck," came an excited voice. "We are having her transported to medical. Captain, you're just not going to believe this."

"Believe what? I'm heading to ship's medical," the Captain told his executive officer. "Keep your eye out for that light."

Heading to the ship's hospital, the Captain encountered the doctor outside the infirmary door. The doctor was just shaking his head.

"Nothing wrong with the child, Captain. She is not even wet. She told me she fell off her father's sailboat and was picked up out of the water by none other than Santa Claus. Then she said he and his reindeer brought her here and put her on our ship. Captain, out in a storm like this, and she is not even wet? She gave me this note. She said it was from Santa Claus."

Opening the note, the Captain read, "This little girl is Jacklyn Billingham. Sailboat Dolphin, with father and two boys, is foundering just over horizon to the east."

The note was signed "SC".

— — —

Once his dad and Billy had been placed in the lifeboat, Thomas struggled across the deck looking for Jacklyn. He could not find her and was surprised to see a gigantic Navy Aircraft Carrier coming up behind them. The ship's rescue boats were already in the water.

"Thank you, Jesus," whispered Thomas. "Please, help me find Jacklyn."

"We've got to find my sister," Thomas yelled to the crew of the rescue boat.

"Don't worry about her, she's fine," a crew member yelled back.

Three seaman boarded the sailboat Dolphin to help get Thomas, Billy, and Todd off the sinking boat and into a litter that would bring them up to a helicopter. Landing on the huge ship's runway, Thomas and Billy were astonished when, after being escorted to the ship's medical facilities, the Captain and Jacklyn were there to meet them.

"Jacklyn, how did you get here?" Thomas asked after their father had been taken into the operating room for emergency surgery on a ruptured appendix.

"Santa Claus," Jacklyn said with a big smile. "I got to fly with Santa and his reindeer way up in the sky, and he brought me to this big ship. I told them that Daddy was very sick, and they said they would take care of him. I don't think they believed me when I told them Santa Claus brought me here." All Thomas could do was look at his sister in awe.

Todd had his operation in the ship's hospital and was delivered to the children's grandparent's home for recovery that evening. Thomas stayed with his father while the rest of the family went to evening services to thank Jesus for delivering their family by way of a helicopter from an aircraft carrier. Secretly all of the family also said "thank you" to Santa Claus for helping bring a wonderful Christmas to the Billingham family.

Santa finished his delivery of presents to all the children around the world, but decided that he needed to make one more delivery. Returning to the Billingham's home, he placed a single present under the small Christmas tree in the living room.

When the Billingham family returned a week later, they found a single box under their tree, addressed to the entire family. Opening the present, they found a plaque reading: "ALL YOU HAVE TO DO IS BELIEVE."

A CHRISTMAS PRESENT FROM MY FATHER

I had been working for my father for a year now. I finished high school at age seventeen and decided that I was not going to go back to school right away and took the summer off. When my father asked me if I had finally made up my mind where I wanted to go to college, I told him I had decided not to go for a while. I was going to take a complete break from school. Of course, he was disappointed, but when I asked him for a job on Christmas Day, he said "yes" without a second thought.

I thought I would work for him for the following summer and then go back to school. Working for my father was something I was looking forward to. I was lucky because I got paid almost as much as other workers who had been with him for many years, but then the other employees weren't their boss's son!

Once I got started, things didn't work out the way I planned. I often wondered what made my father put me on every miserable job there was on his construction projects. My first job was doing nothing but pulling nails out of used lumber for several weeks. One day as he walked by, Dad stopped and watched as I struggled to pull nails out of some old 2x4's he was trying to save for another job.

"You know, Patrick, if you put a wedge under the hammer, raising it a few inches, you will find that those nails will come out a lot easier."

Then he walked onto a different part of the job. Taking a piece of wood and sticking it under the hammer, I found that the nails did indeed pull out easier. I wondered why none of the other workers had not told me this before. I graduated from pulling nails to going from one building project to another pulling and stacking lumber off trucks. It was hard physical work, but it was keeping me out of school, and I was making enough money to buy myself a car. When the market for new homes slowed down, I got the boring job of picking up after the other workers, and this job lasted for several months. I hated the job, but my father wouldn't put me on any other type of work.

I took the winter off when work stopped, but did not go back to school. The following summer, my father had me mixing concrete in a cement mixer for projects in areas that weren't large enough to call in a cement truck. I had to carry the heavy buckets of concrete by hand if we couldn't get the mixer close to where it had to be poured.

On one of the homes, a carpenter had set a frame on the ground that needed to be filled with concrete to support an air conditioner. When the frame was full, I was supposed to smooth out the top of the concrete. Taking a small piece of lumber, I worked over the surface to level it out. My father was walking by and stopped. Watching me struggle to get the job completed, he looked down at me and said, "You know, son, if you take a piece of lumber that goes all the way across the frame, you might find that you can smooth out the concrete a lot easier." Without saying another word, he moved on to another part of the project.

Of course he was right, and I found the job took only a matter of minutes to complete. Why was it that my father had to be the one to tell me how to do these jobs correctly? There were plenty of guys around the project who could have told me, but not one of them offered to give me a hand or share the wisdom to do it right. But they were not the boss's son. Then my father started having me carry shingles onto the roofs of the houses he was building. I carried those 60 pound bundles up ladders for a month before I asked to be taken off the job.

"I was wondering when you would come and ask me if there wasn't an easier way to get the shingles up there," he said.

Taking me aside, we made a lift out of 2x4 lumber with a pulley system that could be propped against the roof of the house. When there was a worker on the roof, all he had to do was take the shingles off the lift when I pulled a bundle up to him. Before, I had to climb a ladder with the shingles on my shoulder. This new method was sure a heck of a lot easier! I still had to pull them up, climb the ladder, and take them off even if there was no one to help me. Thank God that job only lasted for a few months before bad weather set in and the work stopped.

My father had me do every difficult and dirty job there was, and when I complained, he would just smile.

"Be thankful you even have a job since you decided not to continue your education. Not one of the jobs you are doing is one I haven't done myself. It was the way I learned, and it will be the way you learn." By the end of that second summer, I was ready to quit.

It was just before Christmas when I said, "Dad, I've had enough. I'm going off to make my own way in this world. I don't need to work for you anymore. I need to find my life. I'm 19 years old and ready to face life my own way. I feel like I haven't learned a thing about what you do. You build houses by the hundreds, but all I've learned to do is every dirty job you have."

"Okay," said my father. "I will not complain about you quitting your job, if you do something for me. I want you to leave on Sunday and go live with your Uncle Burt on the farm for a year before you go off on your own. Will you do that for me? You do that, and I will also get off your back about continuing your education. You've got my word that I will never say another thing about you going back to school, if you will do this one thing for me."

"Dad, Sunday is Christmas Day. I don't want to go down there on Christmas. I'll miss everything. You know Christmas is a special fun time for me."

"No, son. That's the deal. If you want me off your back, then you have to go and live with your uncle Burt for one full year. All your life, I thought I gave you what you needed but, it looks like I have missed something. This Christmas I want you to give me something I need.

Your Uncle Burt and his family still live in the house where we grew up. You'll love it down there on the farm. Sunday morning you leave," my father said as he walked away.

Christmas was always a happy time for our family, and I had already told everyone what I wanted them to give me. I never let any of them choose my gift. I always had specific things I wanted and insisted that they get, for me, only what I wanted for Christmas. My Uncle Burt! Oh, man! I had not seen him since I was ten years old. He was a "fire and brimstone" preacher in West Virginia. Sure, I went to church all the time with my family — when I didn't have something better to do, but I remembered when he stayed with us for a week, he scared the heck out of me.

I didn't want my father thinking that I did not care about him or that I was never going back to school. I was, just as soon as I got around to it. I just wasn't ready to start back right now. In order to keep my father and my family happy about my decisions in life, I agreed to stay with my Uncle Burt for one year.

When I departed, my father insisted that I ride the bus all the way to West Virginia. He said it would be a good experience for me since I wanted to see the world. I wanted to drive my car, but he said that was not part of the deal.

The trip was okay, except that I had to sit next to a guy who did nothing but talk about how hard his life had been in Minneapolis, going from one homeless shelter to another in that cold part of the country. Now he was going home to bury his mother. Sure, I felt sorry for the guy, but what did his problems have to do with me?

Arriving in West Virginia, my uncle met me at the bus station. When we arrived at the farm, I was surprised at the old house my father had grown up in. It was okay, as far as farmhouses went, but it wasn't anything like the big fancy houses my father built or even like the house we lived in. I have to say my uncle wasn't the "fire and brimstone" guy I remembered. Instead he was a kind man and had a family that consisted of seven others: two girls, four boys, and my Aunt Martha. All nine of us would now be living under one roof. This was going to be my family for the next year! "Oh, give me strength," I thought.

A small building, I guess you could call it a bunkhouse, was off to the side of the main house. It was more like a modern one-room shack where the four boys slept. There was an extra bed where I would be sleeping while my oldest cousin was away at college. The family was poor in my estimation. I would even go so far as to call it "dirt poor," and I soon realized that they did not know how bad off they really were.

After their Christmas vacation was over, all my cousins went back to school with such enthusiasm that it was unbelievable. When they got home after school, the girls helped with supper, but only after they finished their homework. The four boys also did chores, but their school studies always came first, and then they did their chores.

Brad was the youngest at sixteen. He wanted to be an Air Force pilot. Timothy was seventeen and had his heart set on going to the police academy in Chicago. Tommy, eighteen, was the school football star and wanted to try out for a major college team. Charles, at nineteen, had just started his second year in college studying to be a teacher. The girls already had plans for what they wanted to be when they got older, although Elda, the youngest, had changed her mind several times. Me, I had no idea what I was even doing in West Virginia.

What amazed me about the whole family was that they were so poor. As minister of the local church with a congregation of only 600 people, my uncle barely made enough to keep his family alive much less send my cousins to college. I guess that was also why he had the farm. This was a hard life. I would stay the year with my uncle and his family, but I was not going to like it, and I was going to leave as soon as my year was up.

With my Uncle Burt being a minister, I never missed Sunday services. My Aunt Martha would pile all the kids into the van, and since I didn't have a car, I had to ride along with them. The kids had the same eagerness for church as they did for doing their school homework and their chores around the farm — the same enthusiasm for having their chance to say a prayer at breakfast or dinner. Yes, they actually prayed at breakfast and dinner, not like my family in the city who couldn't get out the door fast enough because of all things they had to do. Except for my mother and father, that is. They never missed the chance to thank God for one thing or another.

My mother and father always said prayers at both meals, but my brother, my kid sister, and I were gone most of the time. All of us believed in God and Jesus' salvation, and my parents were very active in our church, but I could never really get into it. There were always other things I wanted to do. When we said a blessing at dinner and I happened to be there, I always had other things on my mind and never paid much attention to what was being said.

My father had given me a Christmas present, as he called it, and I would have to stick it out, but I sure wasn't happy about the deal. My new family was strange, because it seemed as if God was always in the middle of their lives in one way or another. It wasn't as if they were fanatics about it, but God never seemed to be too far away. It was just something I was going to have to get used to.

As the weeks passed and I became bored, I heard my uncle mention to Tommy that there were some hay bales that needed to be put into the barn. I had not spent any time out there, so I thought I would go and see the few animals the family kept. When I entered the barn, I saw Tommy trying to pull a bale of hay up a ladder and into the loft. After watching him for a few minutes, I could stand it no longer.

"Look Tommy, you might be the greatest football star in the world, but you are doing this job all wrong. I'll help you with those now, but tomorrow I will show you how to make a lift so you can get those bales of hay up there by yourself. What we need is some lumber and a few pulleys."

Going back inside the house after we were finished, Tommy was smiling like crazy.

"Tommy, I thought you were going to get the hay up in the loft this evening," my Uncle Burt said.

"All done, Father. I got some help from Patrick. Didn't take long at all, thanks to him."

"My, the Lord does work in mysterious ways, doesn't he?" said Uncle Burt.

The following day, after Tommy had finished his school work, we found the lumber we needed, along with four pulleys, and a long rope. It took us the rest of the evening to get the lift ready for a trial run. All we needed were the hay bales. When we went in for dinner, Tommy asked Uncle Burt to order 40 bales of hay. All his father did was laugh.

"Son, it is going to take you a month to get that much hay up into the loft, and it will only get in the way down in the lower part of the barn."

"No, Dad. Patrick and I will take care of it tomorrow," was all that Tommy said.

My Uncle Burt looked at Tommy for only a few seconds before he said, "Okay, I'll order them for you."

Uncle Burt didn't ask why Tommy wanted so much hay all at one time when he knew it would be in the way until it was placed in the loft. He also didn't ask how he was going to get it up into the loft in such a short time. He just listened to his son and trusted that what my cousin told him would get done.

The following day, I was ready to get started and told Tommy that he could wait on his homework until after we had finished.

"Patrick, I don't know what is important in life to you, but I know what is important to me. Father taught me that first comes how I feel about God and myself. Second, is how I feel about my education and the family I will have in the future. Father says that God just wants me to have my priorities straight."

I looked at Tommy as he walked toward the house. Okay, he just had different views than I did. That's okay, it was just the way my cousin thought. But, that day Tommy got me looking at my own priorities.

It took Tommy only an hour to finish his homework before he walked up and said, "Now, I am ready to see if this lift of yours works."

His comment made me a little nervous because he was trusting that I knew what I was talking about. All I could think of at the time was, "Thank you, Dad."

I'll have to say that it was not easy to carry 40 bales of hay over to the lift. But Tommy and I worked together, and when we were done, we were both proud of what we had accomplished. I was also proud of my cousin because it was not easy to take the bails off the lift and stack them in their proper place, but he never quit. When we entered the kitchen and sat down at the table for supper, my cousin had a big smile on his face.

"Well, how many of those bails did you boys get into the loft?" Uncle Burt asked Tommy.

Still smiling, all Tommy said was, "They're all up there, Father."

Uncle Burt smiled when he looked at Tommy. "So that contraption you boys made really worked, did it?"

Tommy was not surprised at his Father's response. "Yes sir, it did. I told you it would." Looking over at me, he said, "Thank you."

"The Lord does work in mysterious ways," Uncle Burt said again, then looking at me, he added, "Sending you to us for Christmas was His doing, you know."

Uncle Burt was a preacher so what he said didn't surprise me. As the year went on, I taught Tommy and the other boys all that I had learned from my father. My cousins continued to teach me that they were rich in love and kindness not only to each other, but to everyone.

Six months before my year was up, Tommy and I finished putting up a new fence, only this time, it was showing me a few things about running fencing wire.

"Have you gone out to see the farm?" asked Tommy

"No, I have pretty much hung around the farmhouse," I said.

"You have missed so much," said Tommy. "Tomorrow is Saturday, and I'm going to ask Father if we can take you around to see it. I can't believe you haven't seen the farm."

"What's to see, it is just a little farm."

"If Father says 'yes,' we'll take the horses out." I noticed that he had a funny look on his face.

I had been around the horses on the farm, but had never done a lot of riding. The boys often took off on Saturday and stayed out all day, riding up and down the roads around the farm, but because I was not a very good rider, I always declined when they asked me to go along.

"I don't think it's a very good idea. I'm not a very good rider."

"You'll do just fine. We'll go slowly," Tommy told me.

All of us got up early the next morning and left just after breakfast. Two hours later we were riding down a dusty dirt road when I asked Tommy, "Where does your farm end?"

"See those mountains over there? Our farm ends on the other side of them."

I couldn't believe what I had just heard. The mountains looked as if they were miles away. "Tommy, how big is the farm?"

"30,000 acres, but most of it can't really be farmed — too many mountains and streams. Father leases out most of the good farming land. He also leases out the coal mines. Timber is a pretty big deal around here, too.

There is a lot going on around the farm, and Father spends his time keeping track of it."

"It's more like an empire than a farm," I said, still amazed at all I was learning about this place.

"It's always been called `the farm' for some reason. I'm surprised that you don't know much about it since your father owns half of it."

"He told me he owned half of a farm, but I was always too busy doing something else to pay much attention. I was never interested in anything that had to do with a farm."

"Our families don't make a lot of money off it. Most of the profits go to one charity or another and will for the next hundred years." Tommy looked over at me for a few seconds before he continued. "So that's probably why Uncle Bill sent you here. He must have thought it was about time you saw what his family was doing in the world."

"Let me tell you how the story goes. When Uncle Bill and Father inherited the farm from Grandpa, they did not want to be tied down and unable to do what they wanted. So, they set it up where my father could do what he wanted, which was saving souls, and Uncle Bill did what he wanted by going out into the world and making his own way. Sounds kind of like a fairy tale, doesn't it?"

"Well, by setting things up so charities receive most of the proceeds from the land, our fathers can still make a living, save enough to pay for their children's education, and get to do what their hearts lead them to do: to serve God. Father said it started on Christmas Day when he was just a young man. He realized that serving God right here was just as good as going somewhere else, so he decided to stay on the farm and take on the responsibility of watching over it."

After that day, the farm was no longer the same to me. I looked at my uncle Burt and my cousins in a different light. It also had me looking at my father in a different way. I could not help myself. It was as if something had changed in me that I couldn't understand. Uncle Burt and my cousins were so rich in God's love that it overwhelmed everything else.

I rode around the farm a lot with Tommy. I still couldn't fully understand his thinking, but I knew he believed that everything he saw was a reflection of God's handiwork. The dreams he had for his life made me want to look at my own life.

As Christmas drew near, the activity around the farm increased. Farmers who had rented land around the farm, dropped off fresh food, canned goods, meats, and much more. People all over the area stopped by to visit, not only farmers and their workers, but merchants and even the owners of the mines. School students and teachers from several counties stopped to extend their thanks to my uncle Burt and his far away brother. Every individual in my uncle's parish as well as others from miles around must have been grateful for what the farm had done to help them. Tommy said it was like that every year at Christmas.

"Father does not expect to receive Christmas gifts from those he helps, nor does your own father. Everything they receive, they give to the food shelves in the surrounding counties, but not in the name of the farm. They give to all those in need, at Christmas, in the name of God."

"What are you going to ask for at Christmas, Tommy?" I asked.

"Ask for something at Christmas? Why in the world would I do that? Christmas is not about asking for anything. Christmas is about giving."

"I always get what I want for Christmas. I tell my family what I want, and they get it for me," I said.

"It doesn't even sound like you have a Christmas to me! Why not just tell them what you want during the year and forget Christmas? It will mean about the same thing. Patrick, Christmas is about giving all the love you have to others. Whether it's a carved animal like I give my father every year or a four-year paid college tuition like my father gave me last year. I did not receive more than I gave my father, and my father did not receive less by what I gave him. Each of us gave our love to each other."

What could I say?

"Well, I do want something," Tommy said. "That is for my family to be healthy and for all of us to be together at Christmas. But mostly, I want the gift that God gave to us — the gift of salvation. I know it might sound a little corny to you, but not to me."

Uncle Burt had taught his children to believe in God, just as I had learned from my father. The difference was that my cousins lived a life that reflected Christ, while I had been too busy with other things. I learned a lot in my year at the farm. Not about life as I had thought I wanted it, but about the life God wanted for me. I found that my uncle's family was poor in some ways, but extremely rich in so many other ways.

My departure from the farm was not as easy as I thought it was going to be. Everyone was at the bus station to wish me a safe trip home and asked me to come again often. I knew I would miss the family I had just spent an entire year with. I also knew I wasn't going to miss the farm itself, but what it stood for and the way of life it represented.

It took me two days to get back to Minneapolis, and I arrived back home on Christmas Day, exactly one year from the day I left. Father met me at the station.

"Well, did you have a good year on the farm, Patrick?"

"Yes, Father, actually I did."

He looked over at me because I had always called him Dad. The ride home was mostly silent between us. My father must have guessed that I had a lot on my mind, and all his questions would be answered when the time was right. He had always been a model of patience with his two sons. I wonder why I had never seen that in him before.

When I entered the house, the first thing everyone wanted to know was what I wanted for Christmas, since I had not informed them ahead of time. They were surprised when I said I did not want anything because last year, Father had given me the best Christmas present of my life, and it would last me a lifetime.

My father looked at me and smiled. "I told you that you would like it down there. Are you going to be ready to go to work when the weather gets better?"

"Sorry, Dad. I'd love to, but I can't. I'll be in school."

"I can't see where I'm going," Paul told his wife, Alice. "I just can't seem to get out of this blinding snow."

"Can you go lower?" she asked.

"No, it would be too dangerous if we can't see the ice below."

"How far north are we?"

"I don't know. I can't even tell which direction we are flying. Our instruments are going crazy. Try the radio again," said Paul. "We've got to reach someone to let them know we're in trouble"

Alice tried the radio for the fifth time, and she heard nothing but static just like she had been hearing for the last hour. Paul and his family had left Point Barrow, Alaska two hours earlier. They had finished delivering presents to children whose parents did not have enough income to buy gifts at Christmas. Now the aircraft was only half full, and the rest of the presents were due to be dropped off at Wainwright, their second Christmas stop. Once they were delivered, Paul and his family would return home to Anchorage, Alaska.

Paul thought about himself acting as if he were a Santa Claus. As a young boy, he had never believed in that fat, old guy in the red suit who so many called Santa Claus, Kris Kringle, and a few other names. Like his father, he did not believe in Christmas, birthdays, or holidays of any type, and he certainly didn't believe in

Jesus or God. Paul would always remember his father's words, "Jesus and Christmas are nothing but commercial gimmicks to get people to give money to the church or buy toys at Christmas."

Eventually, after hearing his father's remarks so many times, Paul began to think the same way. As a boy they had no tree or Christmas decorations, or mention of God's Son. Eventually, he came to believe in nothing but himself. He didn't celebrate his own birthday much less those of his children — beliefs that caused a lot of heartbreak for his two sons and daughter.

"Christmas is not a time to think about some fat old man who comes along, dressed in red, bringing presents at Christmas," he had told his children many times. This all made a lot of sense to him, especially since he did not believe in God. His own father's words had followed him into his adult life, and he was now saying those words to his own children. That is, until he really found out what God and Christmas were all about.

As his children grew, Alice tried to talk some sense into him, but he would never listen. However, over the last year he had begun to learn a few things about the real meaning of Christmas. Even then it was only after his children had badgered him into going to church with them.

Paul got so tired of hearing about Jesus and God that he finally said to his children, "If I go to church one time, do you promise to drop the whole matter?" Paul even asked Alice for the same promise. Reluctantly all of them agreed.

Paul had not been in a House of God since he was a teenager. Out of curiosity, he had slipped into the side door of a church one Sunday morning just to see what it was all about. Like his father, he did not think too much about it. But one year, because of his children, he went to church the Sunday before Christmas with the family. He certainly did not know what to expect. His children Richard, nine, and Bryan, eight, and daughter, Heather, seven, loved their church especially at this time of year. Alice and the church had taught Paul's children to believe in Christ, and Alice had also taught the children to believe in the goodness of Santa Claus.

Paul knew all he had to do was go to church with his children just once, and the whole matter would be over. However, the second Paul walked in with his family, he immediately knew something was different. The first thing he sensed from all around him was the joy they were feeling as they came together to celebrate Christ's birth. Paul also heard about a lot of projects to help those in need. Dozens of people walked up to him, shook his hand, and said "welcome". This church was not only full of love for Christ, but full of love for all those around them.

Walking out the door after services, Paul felt, for the first time, that maybe he had been missing out on something his whole life. He wasn't sure just what it was, but the feeling would not go away. In fact, it was so strong that Paul decided, just maybe, he would go back one more time, but that would be it.

That one more time, turned into two, then three, then months of sitting and listening to teachings from the scriptures. The words of Jesus were slowly capturing his heart. However, Paul was not fully convinced there was such a thing as God, because he had so many questions that were still unanswered.

As he attended services, Paul began to understand there was something else in life besides having a career and making a lot of money. Paul had made his share of wealth, but was now starting to wonder if he should have shared some of that wealth with others, with his kids on their birthdays, or on special occasions. Maybe even at Christmas.

Paul learned about the sacrifices Jesus had made for him and his family, but he was never truly satisfied by the answer, "All you have to do is believe." He was learning something else — so much of Jesus' teaching had to do with how he should live his own life and how he should have been relating to his family.

In the last year, Paul had been feeling so much different and now actually enjoyed attending services. He was beginning to feel good about himself, but also started to experience guilt about his past behavior. So Paul decided to load up his corporate airplane with gifts to take to the children in the most remote village of the state. It was Paul's hope that by taking presents to the top of the world, his children would forgive him for being so bull headed about birthdays, Christmas, Jesus, and God.

Paul flew his aircraft another hour, knowing he would have to find someplace to land. The plane still had many hours of fuel left, so that was not the immediate problem. He just wanted to get his family on the ground so that they would be safe.

In the months of going to church, he had never prayed. Others around him would, even Alice and his children knew how to pray, but he could never find the words himself.

"Jesus, I don't know how to pray. So, I'll just say a few words the best I can," Paul said.

Alice looked over at Paul and smiled. "Just talk to Him," was all she said.

Paul started slowly and used only a few words in his first prayer to God. "I know I have been gone my whole life, and if you're mad at me, please don't take it out on my family, because I'm trying." Alice again smiled, but said nothing. Paul had come a long way in such a short time.

Looking out the left window of the plane, Paul saw a flash of light go by and disappear to their front. Suddenly he and Alice could see clear sky.

"Well, maybe it is not open ahead," Paul thought as the bottom of the clouds started to drop downward toward the ice. He lowered the nose of the plane, and headed directly toward the opening that continued to get smaller. He was hoping to find a place to land before it closed completely.

"Look," Alice said. "Do you see that large flat area? It looks like we can land there and wait out the snow."

After the aircraft touched down on the ice, Paul saw that the open area was not long enough for him to land the plane and was about to head back into the air. Suddenly, the flat area extended itself out for at least another mile.

"How can that be?" Paul thought as he brought his aircraft to a stop. "I know I saw snow piled up as high as a small hill, then it was suddenly gone. I must have only thought I was seeing all that. I guess it really doesn't matter as long as the plane is stopped. Thank you, Jesus, for saving my family. Look at me. I actually talked to Jesus without thinking about it!"

"What are we going to do now?" Alice asked.

"The only thing we can do is wait for the snow to stop and for it to clear up. Are you three okay back there?" Paul asked the children.

"We are all fine, Dad," answered Richard.

Paul knew that Alice had been checking on the children every minute of the flight since they got caught in the snow, but he had to reassure himself that they were doing alright.

"Bang, bang, bang," came a sound from the side of the aircraft.

"What in the world is that?" asked Alice, startled.

"I have no idea," Paul replied as he looked out the plane's window. "I don't see a thing."

"Bang, bang, bang," came the sound again.

"Dad, I can see someone outside. He looks like a 'Little People' with a beard," Richard said.

"What do you mean, 'Little People'?" asked Alice.

"Like they have on TV. 'Little People', only this one has hair all over his face like Uncle Andy."

"I can see him too," said Bryan. "He is a 'Little People'."

"I want to see too," Heather said.

"You have to keep your seat belt on until Dad tells us we can take them off," Bryan told Heather.

"Not fair," was Heather's response.

"Bang, bang, bang," came the sound again. "Bang, bang, bang."

"I'm going to see what's going on," Paul told Alice.

Paul left the cockpit and went back to the plane's rear door looking out the windows on the way. He did not see the so called "Little People" with the beard, but he did see dozens of small men and women out on the ice. Opening the door, he saw at least a hundred little people, all dressed in unusually lightweight clothing. Many of them had on short sleeve shirts, and no one had on a jacket. The most surprising thing was that they all had really large pointed ears.

Then Paul saw the one with the beard. "We thought you were never going to open that thing up. Come on!

Get the rest of your family and let's go. Our break is almost over, and we have a lot of work still to do. We are sure glad you got here, because without you, I'm not sure we will be able to finish on time. So many requests came in this year, and we are short- handed," said the bearded little man.

Alice and the three children crowded behind Paul as he stepped out of the aircraft. They thought it was going to be freezing outside, but they found that it was quite warm.

"What in the world is going on? As warm as it is, I would think the ice would melt," said Alice. As she spoke, all of the small people turned at once and started to walk away.

"Hold it! Go? Go where?" Paul asked the bearded little man.

"To work. We have a lot of toys to put together, and we can use all the help we can get. My name is Mr. Hanselwing, and I'll show you where you'll be stationed."

"Who are you people?" Paul asked.

"Well, I'm Mr. Hanselwing, and I am the Number One Toy Supervisor of Santa Claus' helpers. I get to decide where everyone will be stationed on the toy line, and I know just where I will put you and Alice. I have a fun job for Richard, an easier job for Bryan, and a fun, easy, job for Heather. Hurry up! We do not want to be late. We only have a week to get the orders ready."

"Toy line? What do you mean toy line?" asked Paul.

Mr. Hanselwing took a big breath. "Look Paul, Santa did not bring you here to his village to just sit around. He brought you here because you did not believe in him. He thought that if you got a little 'toy-action' under your belt, you would have a better understanding about what it feels like to be a real Santa Claus. Santa is giving you his own Christmas present. Come on! You and your family will love being here with us this whole week before Christmas."

Paul turned and directed his family back toward the airplane. He was not sure what was going on, but the safety of his wife and children came first. Reaching the spot where the plane had been, he found that it had been transformed into a beautiful window of color, with images of a toy line in an ever-changing rainbow. Mr. Hanselwing just smiled.

"Beautiful, isn't it? Wait till you are standing on the toy line. You will not want to leave here ever. However, Santa said you and your family can only stay with us for a week. Come on, stand on the line with us. You think you have learned something by being in church for a year? Wait until you see what Santa's boss is going to teach you next."

Paul, Alice and the kids reluctantly followed Mr. Hanselwing across the ice. What choice did they have? As they walked along, Paul was trying to figure out what Mr. Hanselwing meant by "Santa's boss". He was surprised again when he saw the faint outline of colorful buildings suddenly appear out of nowhere. With each step, the buildings became a little clearer. The kids were excited; Paul could tell that they were happy because they were jabbering like crazy. He saw with each step they took, their eyes opened a little wider. Alice was holding onto Paul's hand so hard that he felt she would never let go. When he glanced at her, he saw the biggest smile he had seen since the day Heather was born.

Santa's village was like a workshop wonderland. Paul would go into one building, only to see another just beyond. Mr. Hanselwing said they were short of help, but Paul saw hundreds of Little People in every building. Several small men and women escorted Alice and the children in one direction, while Mr. Hanselwing took Paul in another.

"Your station will be here next to me. What we are looking for is any toy that might have gotten damaged along the way. See that train right there?" Mr. Hanselwing reached out his hand and took a small train off the line. Paul could see nothing wrong with it.

"See that little scratch on top of the smokestack?" Paul looked again and saw a small scratch about a quarter inch long, hardly big enough for him to see unless he squinted his eyes. "It must have gotten bumped somewhere along the line. This will have to be repainted. We do not allow any damaged toys to leave Santa's Village."

Paul spent the day alongside Mr. Hanselwing. Alice was on the next line and close enough for Paul to see. In fact, he could see Richard, Bryan and Heather in the other buildings. It was as if they were also standing right next to him. When Paul asked Mr. Hanselwing about it, the small man just shrugged his shoulders.

"Not our way to take the children out of the sight of their parents. You and I will be able to see them every minute they are on the toy line. They sure are having fun, aren't they?"

The week went by quickly. Paul, Alice and the children got to go onto different lines to see how Santa's helpers were able to produce so many toys for all the good boys and girls of the world. For Richard, Bryan and Heather, it was like being in a department store wonderland with bright colored toys moving along from one place to another.

Paul found that he loved working on assembling the toys while Richard liked painting them. Bryan and Heather liked thinking up new games for next Christmas season. Alice loved everything that was going on around her.

It was one day before Christmas when Santa Claus came in to see Paul. He had just finished building a doll house, and felt really good about how it had turned out. He was placing it on the toy line for painting, when a voice behind him said, "Well, Paul, how do you like our little operation here?"

Turning around, Paul looked into the eyes of the most picture-perfect Santa Claus he had ever seen. He found himself speechless. Why was he so surprised that there was a real Santa Claus, after what he had seen during the past week?

"It has taken me a whole lifetime to understand what Christmas was all about," was all that Paul could think to say.

"Actually. that is not your fault. The boss figured you would come around someday. However, it is most important that your children continue to know that I do exist. We need to break that chain that has held you back from believing. Your young ones already know my boss exists. You know Who I mean don't you?"

"You mean God?" Paul answered. "What you had me doing this past week was for me, as much as my family. They already believe in Jesus, and you needed to show me that you and God really do exist too. Kind of an extreme way of convincing me, wasn't it?"

"No. Some people, like you, grow up not believing in anything. That is such a shame because all of you have missed so much in life. Christmas is all about love and sharing and celebrating Jesus' birth. This experience has helped you learn the truth. Many more will learn about Jesus through Christmas, and someday they will find that God is the author of it all. My job is to help bring them along."

"By the way, Paul, I was not the one who brought you here. The prayers of your wife and children transported you to my village. They wanted so much for you to understand what the birth and death of Jesus did for mankind. Now, there is still one more thing that you must do, and I will show you what that is before you leave my village."

"I thought Santa's Village was on the North Pole."

"After seeing all of this, what makes you think you are not at the North Pole?" Santa asked, followed by a "Ho, Ho, Ho." Paul did not know what to say. After Santa Claus departed, he realized that he had a lot to think about.

It was the last day and the night before Christmas when Mr. Hanselwing came up to him and said, "Okay Paul, are you ready?"

"Ready for what? To go back home? Yes, I think I am."

"Santa didn't tell you, did he? Well, before you came to us, you were playing Santa Claus to some disadvantaged children in Point Barrow, trying to make up for a lifetime of not sharing. Tonight, you are going to see how the rest of the Boss's plan works by going along with Santa and being his right-hand man."

Like a flash of light, Paul was in Santa's village one moment, then back with his family the next. However, he had memories of a full night of flying around the world and delivering presents. One second he was riding beside Santa watching the reindeer pull them through the night sky. Next, Paul was sliding down a black, sooty chimney, but he never seemed to get dirty.

He saw little children hiding on the top of stairs so they could get a peek at Santa Claus. Santa knew they were up there, and would let out a "Ho, Ho, Ho, Merry Christmas!" before he left.

Once passing a mirror, Paul caught a glimpse of himself: that he looked just like Mr. Hanselwing. "Now, why would I look like that short bearded little man? I even have really long pointed ears," he thought. Paul might have been invisible to the children of the world, but he sure wasn't invisible to himself. "God sure works in mysterious ways," he thought. Not once had Paul worried about Alice and the children because he knew they were in good hands and would be well cared for while he was helping Santa.

Now that it was time to go, the sky was clear, and Paul lifted his corporate plane into the air. The instruments were working fine. In the air not more than fifteen minutes, he saw Wainwright, Alaska below him. "How is it possible?" he thought.

"That was a nice flight," mentioned Alice.

"Nice flight. Is that all you can say? What did you think of Santa's village? As if I didn't know," said Paul.

"Excuse me? Santa's village? What are you talking about, Paul?"

"Santa's village. You, me, and the kids. We were there. We helped Mr. Hanselwing and all the other elves put together toys for the good children of the world. It was wonderful. All of us got to build and paint toys, and Bryan and Heather made up new games. I met Santa

Claus, and he talked to me about what God did for the whole world by sending Jesus to save us from our sins. He taught me how important it was to learn and live by God's words and the teachings of Jesus."

"Paul, this trip must have been a little hard on you! But, I am so happy you have become a believer, and are accepting the words Jesus taught."

"Could it be possible?" thought Paul. "Could I have wanted to believe so much, that I dreamed this all up? No, I was there. I saw Santa's Village. I enjoyed building toys. I could not have just dreamed it all."

The trip taught Paul there was more to life than collecting things and making lots of money. His children were happy helping to make other children's Christmas so much more than it would have been. It had been a success after all. But, the memories of Mr. Hanselwing, Santa Claus, and his village would never leave Paul's memory. Most important, though, was realizing that Santa's boss did indeed work in mysterious ways.

After delivering presents to those poor children in Wainwright, Paul and his family flew back to Anchorage. There were only five days until Christmas, and making preparations for the holiday with a tree and its decorations was much more fun than Paul thought it was going to be. Because there was so much laughter, he and his family hardly noticed the winter cold, as they put up lights on the outside of their home.

"How my life has changed by learning what the true meaning of Christmas is all about," thought Paul.

On Christmas morning, Paul got out of bed and went into the living room of their log home. The fire was already burning, the children patiently waiting for their father. The first thing Paul noticed was there seemed to be more presents under the tree than he thought there should have been. A smile crossed his face as he thought about his children giving each other gifts for Christmas. This would be a first for all of them. "I wonder what that could be?" thought Paul when he spied a small gift with his name on it.

Richard was the first to begin passing out gifts. Walking over to the tree, he picked up a very large package and carried it over to Heather. Bryan was next, and he gave a package to his mother. Heather gave one to me, and I made sure I gave one to Richard. When all the packages were passed out, Heather opened her big present first. It was a beautiful dollhouse. Looking up, she said "Thank you, Santa! It's just what I have always wanted!"

"When did you find time to get the dollhouse for her," I whispered to Alice.

"I didn't, I thought you got it for her."

"No, I didn't, but something sure does look familiar about it."

"Paul, look at Bryan's baseball glove," said Alice. "I saw one just like it someplace, but I can't remember where."

"Hey, I got a new game!" hollered Richard. "Man, this is neat!" Looking on the back of the game, he read aloud, "This new game is for all the children of the world, from Bryan and Heather." Bryan and Heather jumped to their feet and ran over to hug their brother, who was smiling from ear to ear.

"It is our game! Santa used the game we made this Christmas. I thought he wasn't going to use it until next Christmas."

Paul and Alice were stunned. What did the children mean Santa used their game? Walking over to Richard, Alice picked up his new baseball glove and looked inside. There were three initials, "ATO" — her initials and the little swirl that she always used after her signature.

Paul reached down and picked up a very small package with his name on it. Opening it, he found a small cross inside brightly colored tissue. On the back, he found an inscription:

I made this just for you, welcome home!

Mr. Hanselwing

We hope you have enjoyed our Christmas stories.
MERRY CHRISTMAS TO ALL THE PEOPLE OF
THE WORLD

www.ingramcontent.com/pod-product-compliance
Lightning Source LLC
Chambersburg PA
CBHW080902120626
46555CB00008B/2923